The World-Mover

by

George O. Smith

The World-Mover
by George O. Smith

Copyright © 2024

All Rights reserved.

ISBN: 978-93-69079-11-7

Published by

DOUBLE 9 BOOKS

2/13-B, Ansari Road
Daryaganj, New Delhi – 110002
info@double9books.com
www.double9books.com
Tel. 011-40042856

ABOUT THE AUTHOR

George Oliver Smith was an American science fiction author. He was born on April 9, 1911, and died on May 27, 1981. He was also known by the pen name Wesley Long. He is not to be confused with American science fiction writer George H. Smith. During the Golden Age of Science Fiction in the 1940s, Smith wrote for the magazine Astounding Science Fiction. John W. Campbell, Jr., the editor of the magazine, stopped working with him when Campbell's first wife, Doa, left him and married Smith in 1949. Smith kept putting out science fiction books and stories on a regular basis until 1960. During the 1960s and 1970s, when he had a job that needed his full attention, he didn't get as much done. In 1980, he got the first award from the Fandom Hall of Fame. He was a member of the Trap Door Spiders, an all-male literary club. Isaac Asimov's Black Widowers, a fictional group of people who solve crimes, were based on the Trap Door Spiders. Smith mostly wrote about space, like in Operation Interstellar (1950), Lost in Space (1959), and Troubled Star (1957).

CONTENTS

To the present sitting, there were three hundred thousand words in the report on the new transuranic element that Les Ackerman was studying. This took months of painstaking work, but Ackerman viewed his results with satisfaction. To date, the report covered about all that was to be known regarding the physical and chemical properties of this new element; there remained only the nuclear properties to investigate.

Nuclear properties were always left to last. Nuclear bombardment defiled the element and rendered it unsuitable for the undestructive chemical analysis and physical investigations.

So Les Ackerman closed his notebook with a slam and checked the refrigerator. The deuterium-ice—frozen heavy water—for the cyclotron target was in fine shape. He could start at once.

He took both the ice-target and the sample to the big, enclosed room and inserted them in the proper places in the cyclotron set-up. Then he fired up the big cyclotron, and high-energy deuterons bombarded the deuterium-ice target, releasing free neutrons that in turn bombarded the sample.

That was to be his last job for the night; the registering counters would record the radioactivity while he slept, and in the morning the sample would probably be 'cold' enough to handle. He consulted his prospectus in the notebook and checked the bombardment-time for this first nuclear test. One half hour. At the end of one half hour, Ackerman could turn off the cyc and go to bed. The automatic counters would quietly record the diminishing activity of the 'hot' sample.

The click of the counting-rate meter sounded. The first atoms of the sample were being attacked properly. Ackerman nodded to himself, there in the operating chamber, separated from the real activity by solid yards of concrete, water, and paraffin.

Unluckily, Ackerman could not be in the cyc chamber itself to watch. As it was, it would have been no more dangerous for Les to stand in the radioactivity-laden cyclotron room than it was for him here in what all cyclotron mechanics considered more than safe from harm.

As the neutrons raced invisibly into the new element, a tiny, glistening sphere expanded, millimeter by millimeter. It was a strange field of energy, a true freak of Nature. Unpredicted and unknown, it hovered at nine centimeters radius as the sample swallowed neutrons by the uncounted million. It expanded again, slowly, slowly, slowly until the critical proportion of sample and transmuted nuclei was attained.

Then the glistening sphere of energy expanded with an acceleration that drove it to the ends of the infinite universe in a matter of microseconds. Too swift to be seen, to register—if there had been a means of detecting it—and too swift even to leave a trace of evidence on the physical universe.

Its effect, however, was evident to Ackerman. The others who came later saw only what they found remaining. Les was on the spot, and saw the dual effect of the bombardment of Element X by neutrons.

His notebook gave the first sight of unreality. Like a double exposure, or a photomontage, he saw page after page curl up in charred destruction—curling up wraithlike out of a complete and unharmed volume! He saw the solid concrete blocks rave into incandescence—flying in terrible fury out of the unharmed wall; each brick as it exploded separating ghostlike from its unharmed twin. The laboratory exploded in a mighty pillar of flame and fire—rising seventy thousand feet into the sky but mushrooming upward from the placidly unharmed ghostly replica of itself. The light from the explosion was all-blinding, yet the calm moonlight still cast its mellow shadow over the unharmed buildings. The explosion shocked fleecy clouds into falling rain—rain that fell from the serenely existing sky of the other—other—other what?

Ackerman found himself standing on the sterile land that surrounded the laboratory, simultaneously watching the boiling cloud above and the moonlit laboratory below. He was puzzled, somewhat afraid to go close to the possible effect of the nuclear explosion; yet there was the fact that at least in one existance the laboratory was unharmed.

He waited, wondering. The passage of time did not seem to bother him. Previously, Ackerman had been tired, and more than glad that this was the last job of the evening. Now he was far from weary, and the passage of time was difficult to estimate.

He was surprised to see, not too much later, that people were streaming towards the scene. He laughed at one group—a racing column of excellent fire-fighting equipment; the idea of tossing water or chemicals on a radioactive explosion was amusing in a sense. The fire had gone out a microsecond or so after it had started, and if anything were burning now, it was because the stuff had not time to cool down yet. Ackerman could think of nothing more dangerous, however, than to drive a fire truck—or anything else not shielded in lead, water, and concrete—across the scorched area.

He saw his colleagues walking wraithlike and arguing heatedly against the police and firemen. The latter wanted to go in; Ackerman's former mates were waving counters and personal ionization meters at them, trying to explain the danger. The officials were inclined to be skeptical of any danger that could not be seen, but were equally awed by the names of the men who barred their way. At long last a crude circle was drawn on the ground; as the curious folk continued to arrive, the circle was quickly filled and people were standing with their toes across the line.

Ackerman found one of his friends near him. "Crowley!" he called.

Tom Crowley did not hear; he continued to argue with another fellow about Ackerman.

"No," said Ackerman, "I'm here—not up in that cloud!"

"Poor Les," said Tom. "I wonder what happened."

Ed Waters shrugged sorrowfully. "I can't imagine; there was certainly nothing dangerous in what Les was intending to do."

"And we know Les," replied Tom. "He'd not take to doing something off the beam."

"There was certainly nothing off the beam about bombarding Element X with neutrons," agreed Ed Waters. "We've done it before."

"But not with as large a sample. We'll have to be careful in the future about it."

Waters grinned wolfishly. "We'll not toss another cyclotron to the breeze," he said. "We can get a neutron-emitting radioisotope from one of the uranium piles and shove the two together by remote control; it'll save both lives and materiel."

"Too damned bad," said Crowley. "We lost a good man."

"But I'm right here!" exploded Ackerman. He had been standing between them, waving his hands in their faces—and in more than one case *through* their faces. Strangely enough, the trees and the ground were quite solid to Les Ackerman, but his friends were not.

The crowds of the curious came and they went; newspapers, as the hours went on, told Ackerman that he was the victim of a terrible atomic blast, a totally deplorable situation.

Ackerman wondered more about it. Was this death?

It was many hours later, when daylight had come fully and the morning's work was to begin, that Les Ackerman got his next shock. The sterile area was still guarded by Ackerman's friends, making close watch with counters and ionization meters. Yet so far as Les was concerned, the shallow depression of greenish glaze fell in a concave bowl below the surface of a serene and untouched terrain upon which the wraithlike laboratory stood. He termed it "wraithlike" because he could see both the greenish depression and the laboratory, and the other side of the blast-bowl through the laboratory. He could not see through the laboratory to glimpse any of its insides.

Whatever this division was, Ackerman could see a dual possibility, could see either the world of the explosion or he could see the world of peace and quiet.

His shock came as the technicians began to arrive. Then, he blinked. As he was standing beside Ed Waters, he saw Waters' car drive up to the parking place beside the laboratory, saw Ed emerge and enter the building by the main door!

Before he could follow Waters, he saw Tom Crowley enter, too; Ackerman left their counterparts on the edge of the seared area and raced forward with a shout of alarm.

It occurred to him, then, that both men carried personal counters and warning gauges; they would have been warned away from the area if there were any radioactive danger. Ackerman found his hand passing through the door-handle and puzzled over how to get in until he understood that if his hand could pass through the door-handle, he himself might pass through the door. He did, and with some dismay knew that he was walking, not upon the floor of the building but about a foot or so below the floor. With an effort of his will alone Les raised himself; it was disconcerting to know that he was wading knee deep through a solid concrete floor.

He found Waters and Crowley in the cyclotron room. They were looking over the sample critically with heavy magnifiers and making notes. "Thought Les was going to flop here," said Waters.

"So did I. He must have decided to go home after he was finished."

"Don't blame him. I'd have been inclined to set the timers and leave then. Ackerman is a cautious fellow and would wait until the timers clicked off even though he had nothing to do but sit and watch unerring meters. I'd say that Les deserved a good night's sleep. Well, take a hunk off of the sample for the radioisotopists, and we'll carve a bit ourselves for later, then give the remaining piece another banging."

"You carve," said Crowley. "I'll get another heavy-ice target from the refrigerator."

Waters nodded, cut two infinitesimal slices from the sample with a diamond-edged wheel, dropped them into separate containers and labelled them both. Then he re-inserted the sample in the cyclotron set-up and both men went out to give the Element X sample a second shot—according to plan, a longer and more energetic blast.

Vainly Les Ackerman tried to reach them.

He screamed himself hoarse, trying to tell them not to do it—that he had been a one-time victim. Then, in fear and desperation, he saw them leave the cyclotron chamber; he fought and swore against his wraithlike fingers that passed through the sample of death. He clawed ineffectively at it, trying to take it from the coming blast of neutrons. Like the room, the walls, and the men, his hands passed through the cyclotron; through the sample; and through the containing shell. Instinctively he knew that the cyclotron was being fired up, yet his fumbling hands felt nothing of the fifty thousand volt driving power of the Dee plates. He knew instinctively when the storm of the deuterons came to bombard the heavy-water ice. He knew that the resulting neutrons were entering the sample of Element X.

He fumed and fretted; then as his mind cried out in vain, his will slipped and Les Ackerman went down through the floor of the room, he could not reach up high enough even to touch the imminent danger.

He turned and ran, almost crying in frustration.

Near the seared edge of last night's explosion, Ackerman turned to watch. An hour passed—Two—Three.

Whatever had happened before, it was not to happen again. Not this time, at least.

For when Les returned, Waters and Crowley were watching the brief half-lives die out on the counters and making histograms in an effort to predict the safety-time.

Mystified, tired of wondering, and utterly lonesome, Les Ackerman waited in the no-world life between two direct possibilities of man's existance.

It was meaningless to Ackerman; perhaps it was meaningless to Nature herself.

The complete incongruity of it all—and the conflicting evidences were beyond him. Trees and rock and ground were one; the building was there and so was that sere bowl of greenish glaze. At nightfall, his friends entered their cars by the laboratory and drove right through the still-crowding people of the other existence. Waters passed almost through his alter ego, and might have seen his friend Crowley twice—excepting that Waters, unlike Les Ackerman, could not see both coincident pathways of event.

CHAPTER 2

Weary, utterly lonesome, and completely baffled about it all, Les Ackerman finally slept. On the hard ground he slept, loath to leave the scene.

He was awakened by the sound of a voice speaking his name. Shaking his head, Les sat up, saw that it was just about sunrise, and answered instinctively, though he knew that his voice could not be heard. He could hear people—but people could not hear him; just as he could see people but they could not see him.

"I'm right here," he said for, perhaps, the ten-thousandth time. He expected, for the ten-thousandth time, that he would not be heard.

"Good," replied the voice.

Then in the growing light, Ackerman saw a glistening, egg-shaped vehicle coming slowly through the grove of trees. It hovered above him and settled easily to the ground.

The voice, he saw, came from a woman who was obviously driving the thing. There was a small hemisphere of glass thrown back from the 'top' of the vehicle, and the woman was head and shoulders above the level of the hull.

She smiled, and Ackerman was instantly attracted. "Well," she said with an air of successful finality. "You've arrived."

Ackerman shrugged. So far as he was concerned, the girl could get out of the vehicle and make passes at him; he was still as isolated from all people as a butterfly in a glass case at some moldy museum.

"Have I?" he answered, still skeptical.

"You have." She ducked her head down into the vehicle and re-appeared, coming out of a door in the side. He was a little surprised at her clothing. He expected something bizarre; at least she might have been dressed in something in keeping with the completely exotic vehicle she was driving.

But she was dressed in a simple frock of silk or nylon. Tasteful, modern. She was auburn-haired and very attractive according to Les Ackerman's fastidious standards.

"I'm Tansie Lee," she said, offering a slender hand. He took it and found it firm and warm.

"I'm Les Ack—"

"I know; after all, I've come a long way to find you."

"Me?" asked Ackerman in complete wonder.

"You don't really know what happened?" Her tone was teasing, and she was obviously enjoying every moment of it.

"No, not really," he said. "All I know is that I was bombarding Element X with neutrons and then—well, it's rather hard to describe. I can lean against a tree, but I can also walk through the laboratory door. That doesn't make sense."

"Yes it does when you're properly introduced to your environment. Look, Les, you are in the middle, lost territory between two branching streams of events. In one branch, you were the victim of an explosion; in the other, your efforts were successful in the lab.

"Now," she said, groping for the right words so that her explanation would be simple, "a tree might be in both worlds; therefore you can lean against it. If a woodcutter in one branch of events cuts the tree down, then you could walk through it in the other branch. The laboratory is there in one branch only; the green bowl of atomic explosion is there in the other. Follow?"

Ackerman let that digest for a moment and then said: "What would happen if I tried to break off a tree branch myself?"

She laughed. "You'd find—and you'll find—that things consist only of Aristotelian extremes. Either they are non-coincident and therefore very intangible, or you'll find that they are coincident and as untouchable as tungsten carbide to the bare hands. You can walk through non-coincident granite but you couldn't make a dent in coincident tissue paper."

"Then how do my life processes continue? Either I must be breathing coincident—and therefore untouchable and unchangeable air—or I must be breathing non-coincident and therefore untouchable and unchangeable air."

She laughed heartily. "Trouble is, Les Ackerman, you don't really exist; therefore your life processes are unreal."

"Oh—I don't exist, hey? Then what is this that is I?"

"I'll skip the metaphysics," she said with a laugh. "Do you doubt the reality of unreal things?"

"Isn't that a disclaimer in itself?"

She shook her head. "The square root of minus one is an unreal number. It is a pure formulation, and yet it is an important factor. You cannot dig too deeply into any phase of science without using it—and yet it is still an imaginary quantity. It does not truly exist, nor do you. Yet it is there as a formulation, and that is what you—and I should add: I—are, or am, or whichever."

He laughed too, at her confusion. "We are," he said, but it was more of a question than a correction of her grammar.

"We are—and there are and will be others, too."

"But I do not understand it at all."

"It is not to be easily understood," said Tansie. "Not without help. I'll help, if you want."

"I'd be happy to know what the answer is," said Les. "Just how do you propose to help?"

"My machine. Take a ride?"

He nodded. "I'm hungry; have you any groceries in that thing?"

"While we're following the world line," she promised, "I'll show you that I can cook, too. Come on!"

Tansie led him cheerfully into the vehicle and closed the top-hatch. "We'll be heading into space," she said in a matter-of-fact tone.

"Space?" he gurgled.

She nodded.

"But why?"

"In our—condition—being sort of trapped between two world lines, we are swept along in synchronism with the 'temporal advance' of the massive earth. The earth is moving through 'space'. Since we have little free 'temporal inertia', we are instantly drawn to whatever era lies in the physical mass. Follow?"

"Not too well, but it sounds like saying that if the four o'clock train arrives now, it must be four o'clock."

Tansie laughed. "We go to the 'space' where earth will be in a hundred years. Then, having no 'temporal inertia', we are drawn through time to that 'instant'.... You know as well as I do that our language of words and subject-predicate sentences dissects events into artificially blocked-off units like 'time' and 'space'. But these inadequate bits of word-magic make you feel better.... People not trapped in 'free time' are possessed of almost infinite 'temporal inertia' and the natural gravitational attraction between masses is the main activating force."

Ackerman nodded. "I suppose that indicates some sort of intrinsic motion?"

"Not necessarily."

"But all things are relative."

Tansie thought for a moment. "I don't understand."

"If all things are relative, then position must be."

Tansie looked blank. "I'm asking no questions," she said. "But 'time', too, must be relative. And I know that 'time' is relative to 'space', too. The entropy factors change near massive bodies. Why not 'time?' 'Time' changes with velocity, as does mass. 'Time', mass, and velocity are all factors."

"You forgot energy. Velocity is a function of energy, which is interchangeable with mass, which affects the 'temporal strains'. The whole is one—or in less elision, they are all manifestations of one another."

Tansie smiled, stood up from the control of the ship, and beckoned with her thumb. "You're the brilliant physicist," she said. "But I'll bet I can fry a non-existant egg better than you can."

"Mind if I ask where you get these imaginary eggs?"

The girl laughed and tossed her auburn hair at him. "Real hens lay real eggs. There's two possibilities—"

"I know," he said, joining in with her good spirits, "Either we have a gang of 'time-trapped' poultry, or the art of getting 'time-trapped'—along with an icebox full of provender—takes a firm stand somewhere along the line."

"There's means," she admitted.

"Okay," he said. "You cook—and also explain to me just why you seem to think I'm the brilliant one."

"We know you are," she said; "you bear the necessary knowledge to avert disaster."

"Me?"

"You." She pointed at him with a flapjack-flipper, then used it to fracture the shell of an egg. "But no explanation of that right now; it's too consarned complicated. Wait until you learn more about it, and it'll save us all a lot of time."

"But I'm curious."

"Naturally," she said with a whimsical smile. "But I'm going to make the best of this trip, and I don't want to spend every waking hour in explanation; you'd grow tired of me."

The smell of bacon and eggs permeated the place. Les lifted his face and made a show of flaring nostrils sniffing hungrily. The aroma of toast was added, to which was again the odor of butter hitting the hot toast.

"If that tastes as well as it sounds to the nose," he grinned, "I could take a lot of your company."

Tansie whirled the plate before him, placed a cup of coffee beside it. Then she sat across the table from him with her own plate and plied her knife and fork in silence.

He wondered about Tansie; she was singularly receptive to his likes and dislikes, even to the idea of not talking while he was eating. He said nothing until the coffee, and then he looked up and smiled. "That," he said, "was to the taste of Caesar."

She dropped a curtsy that was not well executed because she was not wearing the kind of skirt that makes a curtsy the sweeping genuflection it was intended for. "I render unto Caesar that which is Caesar's."

What stuck foremost in his mind was the fact that Tansie had neglected to supply sugar and cream for the coffee—which might have been a natural gesture—and he wondered whether she knew that he used neither. He did not press the question; he would let more evidence pile up before he accused her of being able to read his mind.

"You'll be interested in a look outside," she said.

"Why?"

"We're not many months ahead, so far. The trees have fallen, and greened again; yet there is sufficient non-coincident growth to make the sight somewhat bizarre."

They went to the control cabin and Tansie slowed the ship until the gray haze outside diminished and the landscape became clear again. The sight *was* strange. Now, instead of coincident trees, only the main branches were single. The leaves were in that 'temporal' double-exposure, since the twin worlds were beginning to lose their twinship, each following its own line of future.

"Weird," he agreed, "but I thought we'd be heading into 'space' for certain."

"We are in 'space'," she said. "So far as true 'time' is concerned. The earth is way back there." She pointed off vaguely in a gesture that embraced a full fifty degrees. "Trouble is that this heap wouldn't spacehop worth a tin cent in real life. But remember, we have little true inertia, and therefore a bit of propulsion does a lot of work against a minute mass. It also is less a matter of protection than convenience. You could get out now if you wanted to."

"No," he said.

"But we will stop to stretch our legs after lunch." That, too, struck Les Ackerman in the right pocket.

Tansie had picked him up at about six o'clock in the morning, and the time between then and the clock's registration of noon was pleasant. The girl was brightly amusing and bafflingly vague as it pleased her fancy. She intrigued Ackerman's interest deeply, and the liking was heightened by the almost certain fact that she knew much more about the thing, but was not telling. There was time, she said. Most of the talk was light, or deliberately kept light by Tansie Lee. It went as follows, or approximately so, depending upon the subject: "But how did you find me?" he asked.

"I knew where—and when—you'd be."

"How did you know?"

"Well, for one thing, it's history."

"Yeah," he drawled, "but whose?"

"The unwritten history of the no-world." She laughed.

"Balderdash."

"Well," she said. "We do not exist; we are not really here. Therefore the history of our lives is also figmentary. It doesn't exist."

"No?"

"Nope," she said with a shake of her head. "Nothing is real."

"Then how do you read facts out of an unreal book?"

"How do you multiply a real unit by an imaginary number?"

"We do it—Oh nuts."

"Okay," she laughed. "It'll all come out in the wash. Lunch?"

"Lunch!" he said firmly.

He led her to the galley and rummaged idly into the cabinets. In one he found a bottle that smelled inviting. "Will this," he asked, holding it up and sloshing the amber fluid in the bottle, "give we unreal people unreal hangovers?"

"It depends," she told him, opening the refrigerator and handing him a tray of ice cubes.

"Depends," he said ruminatively, busily mixing, "Upon the truth of positives and negatives. A real person with an unreal hangover might not feel it any more than I can feel an object that doesn't exist simultaneously. Similarly, we unreal people might not notice a real hangover. But if we unreal folks get unreal hangovers by drinking unreal whiskey, it might hurt. Is that it? Is that what it depends on?"

She took the proffered glass. "Nope," she said, looking at him over the rim of her glass. "It just depends—like as usual—upon how much of this stuff you think you can pack away."

They stopped after lunch, parked the vehicle in a grove of trees and went out for a walk.

"I note that things are single," said Ackerman.

"Wrong," she said. "Look again. Down."

He looked down. Down—through the hard earth to where there was another surface at least fifty miles below. Another ground-plane, dim, unreal, but like the one upon which they stood.

"Why?" he asked her.

"Your explosion was minute, as cosmic powers go. But this is many years later. The most minute deviation will make a difference in displacement after a hundred years. You, my sweet, are a Man Who Moves Worlds." The capital letters were implied by her tone, and the affectionate term seemed to come naturally.

It pleased Ackerman. Tansie was an attractive girl. She was as lost in the middle of the 'time-lines' as he was. Friendship—even love—might come swiftly under attractive isolation, but Ackerman believed that neither the isolation nor the length of time had been great enough yet. The attractiveness was admittedly there.

And something in the back, ignored-because-it-was-unpleasant part of his mind was telling him, vainly, to watch out because this was entirely too idyllic.

Ackerman clapped a lid down on the malcontent thought and reached for Tansie's hand to help her up over a fallen log.

He retained her hand after help was no longer necessary; he liked it. The pleasant contact crowded out the wonder if on the other existance, miles away, had a similar fallen log.

He cast a sidelong look at her, and caught her watching him. They both stopped and faced one another.

Tansie stood there proudly, facing him, waiting. He fumbled mentally for a moment and then blurted: "Tansie. Tansie, what is all this?"

She smiled wistfully. "Not yet," she said. "It all must be. I—am not to tell you yet. And—Les—I'd prefer, even so, not to spoil it."

"Spoil it?" he exploded. "My idea is to get whatever trouble there is to be over with so that I can take the rest of whatever time there is for me to know you better."

"You'll have a lifetime," she promised. "Providing you are a completely free agent. My dear, this way I am sure of the future. One small slip, and the future is changed. You—"

"Baloney!"

Tansie took a step towards him. "Forget it." Her eyes were inviting— He looked into them; Ackerman, in thirty years of life, had never before met the girl whose eyes drew him so.

He reached for her, and Tansie came willingly into his arms. He thought briefly that Tansie could make him forget anything—and was proven right; he forget even that.

CHAPTER 3

Seconds, or seven thousand years later, a rough laugh broke it up. Tansie hurled herself away from him, whirling out of his arms. The other was facing them less than ten yards away.

"Very pretty," he said with heavy scorn. "Very pretty." He waved at them with a carbine. "So the great physicist, the hope of the civilized world, ultimate founder of the galactic empire, is found lollygagging with a broad."

"Listen—" snarled Ackerman. He lunged forward, blind with anger. The loud *crack!* of the rifle brought his head up, and the bullet smacked the ground between his feet.

"What's the matter?" asked the other with an oily voice. "You object to my term? Well—Tansie, you tell him."

Tansie shook her head, dazedly. "You can't say—"

"No?" snapped the other. "Well, I'll tell him, Tansie. Ackerman, your gal-friend is married."

"No—!" cried Tansie in a voice of mingled pain and terror. She was cut off by another crack of the carbine.

Tansie looked at the other man. "Calvin Blaine, you're not—"

"Ackerman is coming with me," said Blaine.

"I don't think so," Les told him.

Blaine laughed cheerfully. "You haven't much to say about this."

Les spat in the other's direction. "Don't let me get within grabbing distance of that gun," he told Blaine. Disdainfully, he turned his back and faced Tansie.

"Is it true?"

She looked at Blaine.

Blaine said, in a cold voice, "Tell him the truth, Tansie—or I'll kill *him*."

Ackerman turned again. "Truth?" he sneered. "Truth at the point of a gun? 'Truth' in this case is forcing Tansie to make a statement that you approve. Truth! Bah!"

Tansie looked at Ackerman, then at Blaine; this was an event she had not counted on. Tansie had believed that the history she knew—unwritten but known—was truth, despite its happening in the future respective to 'Real Time.' She had been wondering about predestination and the resulting futility of all effort; this seemed to prove to her that this nebulous life was still subject to change at the whim of chance. But Ackerman was important, and even though his definition of truth was correct in this case, he must not be destroyed.

She looked at Blaine and then at Ackerman; the collapse of all her hopes had stricken her dumb.

Tears were close to the surface. Tears for herself, for her hopes—and for Les Ackerman. Yet there was a chance. Les must not be destroyed, even at the expense of her own life; Blaine knew that, which was why he threatened Ackerman instead of her.

Calvin Blaine lifted the carbine.

Les Ackerman measured his chances and decided against them, for the moment at least.

With hidden tears stinging her eyes, Tansie Lee held up her left hand. Ackerman looked down and saw it. Very plain, very formal, as lacking in surface glitter as Tansie had seemed—Les wondered whether the simple serenity of the wedding ring was as false a cover for cheap green brass as— as—

You damned fool! he told himself. *You trebly underlined, capital-lettered idiot! A soft glance, warm lips, and an almost-invitation—and you forget yourself!*

The blind, stupid haze cleared from Ackerman's bewildered mind and he looked into Tansie Lee's face. She had been looking at him, searching his face carefully. But she had seen his expression, and was turning away. Ackerman watched her go, coldly. *A fool*, he said to himself, *is a man who makes the same mistake twice!*

Tansie walked away, her shoulders down, her warmly-rich figure gaunt, and the line and soul of dejection.

Calvin Blaine coughed and said: "Sorry, Ackerman. This is mostly for self-defence. I knew she'd work on you very well before I got to you—and I knew that she'd work well enough to drive you into blind fury at the first mention of her perfidy."

"I don't understand all of this," said Ackerman. His voice was hard and his attitude one of complete indifference. "What's going on, anyway?"

"You've heard of two countries, or two men fighting for their lives?"

"Yes."

"Ackerman, you started this. Unwittingly, of course. Bombardment of Element X—which we call *Temperon*—produced a freak field of force that caused a division in the universal stream of time. It has never happened before and it will never happen again according to the probabilities—no one knows what happened.

"This, Ackerman, produced a twin existance. Two probabilities that stem from a dual explosion in your laboratory. In one, there was a complete success to your work; in the other, there was total destruction of your effort. Not only did you split the world into twin existances through 'time', Ackerman, but you also split it definitely into twin camps of reasoning. Your work was based upon findings that came from countries that were enemies not many years before. Figuratively, you stood on the shoulders of scientific wisdom to prepare your manuscript of facts on the element temperon.

"Your work was an indictment of any policy that would hamstring the free interchange of ideas, concepts, work, and success. It was living proof that all men contribute to the advancement of civilization whether they be good, not so good, bad, quick, dead, friend or one-time enemy.

"The other existance, however, has your evidence that men were plodding through the uncharted seas of boundless energy and power—"

"But I was not!" stated Ackerman.

"You know that and your fellows know it. But your scientific fellows are a minority, and many of them doubt their own figures. They know only that *something* blew you and your laboratory off of the face of the earth, and they all wonder why—even those who claim to *know* that you were working with nothing dangerous.

"Therefore, Ackerman, because you and your kind were obviously playing with a field of work that might cause the destruction of the universe, research is throttled and controlled to within an inch of its life. There is no leaping from an unfounded theory to cold mathematics to foregone conclusion like a fast double-play from short to second to first. To bombard a ten milligram sample of anything never before bombarded, the scientist must make ten ten-hour bombardments, adding one milligram each time."

"Well—where do I come in?" asked Ackerman.

"You have the answer to mankind's life in your brain," replied Blaine. "We need your help."

"That's about what Tansie Lee was telling me." Ackerman's mind underwent a very brief session of self-denunciation at the thought of Tansie.

"I'll show you," he said. "My ship is hard by. I'll show you, Ackerman, the destruction of a solar system by men who know too little about the stuff with which they work."

Ackerman shrugged uncertainly. "I'm not Solomon, nor even one of his seventh-assistant helpers," he said thoughtfully. "But it strikes me that there is as much danger letting everybody play with atomic fire as there is in throttling all brainwork."

Blaine laughed heartily. "Any kind of fire," he said between shouts of admiring laughter. "Even firewater! They tried complete prohibition once and people started to make everything from Allyl Acetate to xylylene glycol in their cellars! No one yet has thought of legislation forcing everybody to swizzle a quart a day, and even the flushest of lushes doesn't offer drinks to kids. No, Ackerman, you're to be proven correct."

"Why?"

"That's partly why we need your help," said Blaine. "People have been bootlegging science to a dangerous degree. In the other existence, people have been taking a free and untrammelled holiday. In the future to which we're going, you'll see the answer. Men have learned the folly of fighting one another, Ackerman, but they have also learned the way across the strait of 'time'. Burning up my world by atomics will not cause their own world to die."

"Doesn't that give them both a future?"

Blaine clapped Ackerman on the shoulder and smiled sorrowfully. "They cannot cross materially," he said. "They can blast only with energy. Yet, even so, there is jealousy, hate, and malice. Remember this, Lester Ackerman: what man cannot conquer, man destroys!"

Calvin Blaine's ship was about the same as Tansie's. Blaine motioned Ackerman in and followed, closing the door. From the controls, up in the pilot's deck, came a musical voice that struck a chord in Ackerman's mind: "You found him, dad?"

"My daughter," said Blaine unnecessarily. She came to meet them; a golden blonde with sparklingly mischievous eyes, upturned corners of a round, rich mouth that was also generous, and a warmly tanned skin.

"This is he, Laurie. Ackerman, my daughter, Laurie Blaine."

"How do you do, Miss Blaine."

"I do fine, usually," she told him with a laugh. "And I start at once; you are to call me Laurie; I'll eschew formality, too, and call you Les." She turned to her father. "Are we off in the planned direction?"

"We are. I succeeded in getting to them before any damage was done."

"Soon enough?" asked Laurie with a devilish glint in her eye. Ackerman squirmed uncomfortably, wishing he could duck the double entendre.

Calvin Blaine recognized the possibility of Ackerman's discomfort—possibly because Blaine was no more perfect than anyone else. He would never tell Laurie that he had interrupted a love-scene; she would never know unless Ackerman blurted it out.

He nodded negligently. "He didn't know who she was," he said.

Laurie smiled at Ackerman. "We know that Les Ackerman is a shy man," she said. "It—is becoming. But to tell you the truth, Les, I'd be worried about a bronze statue if that woman decided to hurl herself at its head." The way Laurie said 'That woman' was of the same tone that one uses in describing someone who was violating the 'No Spitting' ordinance in the subway. "You're still pure and simple?" she asked him with a laugh.

"I'm simple, anyway."

"Good; I'm not too bright in some things. Dad's tried to tell me about temperon. I'm baffled; what's temperon?"

Ackerman took a deep breath and was frankly glad to get off of the tender subject of his affections and onto a more stable discussion of material physics.

"It's an involved yarn," said Ackerman. "Back in the nineteen-thirties, a scientist by the name of Enrico Fermi was successful in bombarding almost every element with neutrons, and succeeded in most cases by raising the atomic number of most of them. The neutron, you see, enters the nucleus, making the nuclear mass too great for the nuclear charge. The nucleus then re-establishes stability over a time by emitting a beta particle, transforming, in effect, one of the neutrons to a proton. Now the top of the periodic chart is uranium, and Fermi wondered what he would get if he tried to raise the top-number."

"That was plutonium?" asked Laurie.

"Neptunium first, then plutonium. After the Second War, science took up again, investigating for the sake of learning more about their surroundings. Plutonium was top-number for not too long. Element ninety-five came next, and ninety-six followed soon. We were working on element number one hundred and forty-four; that is the one called temperon."

"There are that many elements above the former top?"

"There are, theoretically, an infinite number of elements. Most of the top elements are unstable—that is, radioactive. Fissionable elements occur more and more frequently in the top brackets. No one has ever seen element one hundred and eight, you know; it fissions automatically as soon as it is made."

"How do you hurdle it, then?"

"Bombard it with deuterons, which raises the charge one number and the mass two numbers. It isn't easy, but it works." He looked at Laurie with curiosity. For an avowed lack of education in atomics, Laurie knew the proper questions to ask. He wondered whether her interest was as great or her desire for knowledge as deep as she said—or whether she were doing her best to put him at ease by leading him into talk about the subject he liked best.

Then, surprisingly, she looked him in the eye and winked with a brazen leer. She stood up and headed for the kitchen, knowing that he would follow. When he arrived, she was busily mixing drinks. He smiled. It was an excellent grade of scotch; he said so.

The drink relaxed him.

Laurie took the third drink in to her father. "Good for the soul," he said to Ackerman, lifting the glass.

"It is," he said heartily.

Then Calvin Blaine drew Ackerman's story out. Blaine was genuinely interested in the true history of the world, and enjoyed listening to Ackerman's description of the events that took place during the World War II and afterwards. "First hand telling," said Blaine. "It held cards, spades, and big casino over the books." The drinks helped Ackerman to relax, and before he knew it, the aroma of fine steak was filling the ship.

Laurie, too, was an excellent cook.

CHAPTER 4

It was, said Les Ackerman as he awoke, an eventful sixty hours since the eventful partial explosion on his laboratory. And in twenty-six hours since Tansie Lee had found him at six o'clock the previous morning, Les had travelled several hundred years and a good many millions of miles in space.

Not bad, he thought, *for someone who does not exist.*

He stretched and turned over for another forty winks, and was dozing when the door opened and Laurie Blaine came in with coffee, which she held temptingly under his nose until he reached for it, and then held completely out of reach.

"Come and get it," she said mischievously.

"I don't dare," he laughed.

"How will I know that you're getting up?" she asked suspiciously.

"Take my word for it; that smells like tomorrow morning."

"Well," she said brightly, "in case you're interested, this *is* tomorrow morning. Get up!"

"You get out and I'll get up," he told her.

Then from the doorway, Calvin called: "Better; we're not long nor far from the scene I want to show you."

"Good enough for me," replied Ackerman. "Drag that woman out of here, will you?"

"Come on, shameless wench," laughed Blaine to his daughter. "Despite your arguments, modesty is a virtue. Let the man get dressed in peace." He grinned at Les. "She'd sit there and make snide remarks about your knees," he said. "Git!" he told her.

She got. And Les was thoroughly awake and dressed in minutes.

After breakfast, Blaine took the controls himself. "We'll watch this from a distance," he said. "I've enough power to break away from the temporal inertia and attractive mass. We can see both sides of this thing, which is more than those doing it can see."

There was the feeling of lift to the vehicle. It went on for an hour, through the gray haze that pressed against the windows of the ship while they were in motion. Then, finally, Blaine turned from the controls and the haze cleared.

"I've accelerated the 'time-rate'," he said. "Now that we're out of the earth's attractive temporal field."

"Why?"

"Destruction of anything the size of the earth takes time," explained Blaine. "I've read stories in which the earth crashed into another planet, and it took place in a matter of minutes. Forgetting that at planetary velocities—earth is about seventeen miles per second orbital, if I remember correctly—it takes the earth over a minute to cover one diameter of motion. Also the chances of a real crash, like a couple of golf balls colliding is impossible."

"Roche's Limit?" asked Ackerman. "They'd start to come apart by mutual gravitational attraction before they hit, and the resulting crash would be more like two spoonsful of baking powder hitting one another."

"Sounds messy," said Laurie.

Ackerman looked cheerfully sour. "It would be," he told her.

"This affair is not to be that simple," stated Blaine. "No collision. Just beamed energy. Equally messy, though."

"The 'time' speed-up is obvious, isn't it?" asked Les, looking at the distant earth through the telescope. "I can definitely perceive the turning."

"We're running free at about twenty to one," said Blaine. "Earth will turn once in about an hour and twelve minutes."

"When does the big show start?"

"Any moment now."

"But where's the green hazy fog?" asked Les. "I thought—"

"That fog is only apparent when near a body like earth. It is caused by the diffraction of the air—you see, when you're moving through 'time', the speed-up of air-motion causes a complete diffraction and diffusion of all light. We're in space where there is no air."

As Blaine spoke, a twinkle of light burst like an exploding bomb a half diameter to the north of the earth. The speckle of light spread and diminished in intensity; it still cast a baleful but momentary glow over the northern hemisphere—or not-quite-hemisphere because of its proximity to the earth.

"That's the beginning," said Blaine.

Minutes later, a second pinprick of energy expanded. This one was either on the surface or very close; it was hard to tell which. But the effect was terrible. A ruddy gout of multicolored smoke and flame spurted out, leaping from the point of contact. It raced up and away from the surface making a tiny tuft of fluffy smoke that looked like a wisp of cotton pulled through the cloth covering of a pillow. It was tiny compared to the size of the earth, but the shock wave that raced in a concentric circle away from the gout of energy—racing across the ground in a crawling distortion—was quite visible. Its amplitude died as it spread until it was invisible.

Minutes later, a contracting circle of shock-wave appeared. It converged and closed down on the spot that was still covered by the tiny cloud. There was considerable amplitude at that spot where all the energy returned, then the concentric shock wave raced away from the point again.

"I'd like to see the antipodes," muttered Ackerman.

"We'll see others," Blaine promised.

"That was the same shock wave, wasn't it?" Laurie wanted to know.

"Yes," said her father, watching through his telescope. "It started from that city and spread out across the earth. On the other side, of course, the thing converged to zero, passed through itself and spread out again. It returned to its origin—and will continue to encircle the earth until it dies. Each time it is less perfect because of wave-diffraction and refraction due to a non-homogenous medium. That tends to spread it out, makes its focal point imperfect. Its energy will be dissipated in heat due to resistance. It will eventually die and—"

"Here comes one!" exploded Laurie. "From the other side."

They watched. The shock wave converged, growing in amplitude as it circled down to the pinpoint. There was a clouding at the focal point where earth itself ground itself to bits in the grip of a transmitted wave of energy. The receding wave spread out again.

Fascinated, horror-stricken, Ackerman, Laurie Blaine, and her father watched the Earth being consumed by atomic fire.

Then, as though the enemy had been searching out their target—bracketing it—other pinpricks burst in widely separated places. The criss-crossing of concentric shock waves cast up high peaks that raced along, tearing up the very ground.

"On earth," said Blaine, "Nine hours have passed since the initial blast."

More time passed, and then with the target accurately bracketed, the pinpricks of energy burst again and again and again in lightning speed. The face of Terra sparkled; scintillated. The ground writhed and boiled; mighty gouts of earth and tortured stone burst upward where the bursts of power drove below the surface. The scintillating face of the earth increased to a constant glow as the ferocity of the attack increased. Moving clouds of gray and white obscured the surface, through which came the angry, flaming glow of surface bombing by high, sheer energy.

The color temperature of the cloud increased until the scintillating, ever-changing illumination changed subtly. Now the smoky, cloudy earth shone with an angry glow more bright than the individual sparkles; it was like a fog-cloud illuminated from behind. "The earth," said Blaine in an awesome voice, "is growing incandescent."

Ackerman took a deep breath. "And still," he sighed bitterly, "they continue!"

"They will continue, until they raise the temperature of the earth so high that the thermal energy is sufficient to exceed the escape velocity of the earth's mass. Then, driven by the power of the light-output, the earth will disperse in a cloud of streaming, incandescent gas. For," Blaine added sardonically, "as the first quantities start to leave, the mass diminishes and the escape velocity diminishes also. The earth will expand in white-hot gas and disperse forever."

"Horrible," said Les Ackerman through a dry and aching throat.

He turned from the telescope and faced Calvin Blaine. "I—started this?"

Blaine nodded, but added: "Unwittingly. No fault of yours."

"Then, what can I do to avert it?"

"You must help us," said Blaine. "Will you?"

"I'll do anything. But if this is an extension of 'Time', how can the future be changed?"

"This is just a most certain probability; intervention may change it."

Ackerman sat down weakly, and was thankful for the oversized jolt of scotch that Laurie handed him. "I'm still puzzled; it seems to me that this splitting-off in 'time' must go on constantly. A tree might grow either to the left or to the right. Do not these offer different world-line endings?"

"By and large," said Blaine, "they do. But you must remember that most incidents are unimportant to the complex. We have two living possibilities due to your unfortunate accident. You see, Ackerman, it is true that a tree may grow either to the left or to the right; it does not grow both ways. When the 'time' comes for the decision to be made, the forces that work toward causing that decision have been in force for some duration and the tree takes the most logical move; therefore only one future ensues. Even in the decision of a possible dictator of all humanity, the decisions he makes are dependent upon his past experience. Grand Chance is not a matter of tossing dice; men have a free will, Ackerman. Yet their lives are fairly well cast ahead of time by the course of their pasts. The formula that caused World War II to grow out of World War I was evident enough to prevent World War III; yet in no way could Adolph Hitler have been averted because he rose out of a situation already created."

"It still sounds like predestination—and the futility of all effort."

"Not so. You are a free will, Lester—yet your actions are conditioned by your past. By 'free will', I mean you have a choice of alternatives within the frame of conditions around you. The only ones whose actions are not dictated by solid experience are the insane. And they, even by the Ancients, were termed 'Unpredictable'."

Ackerman nodded. Once you knew a man, you could make a fair prediction of how he would react to a given set of conditions, starting no major alterations in his motives and view points, etc. Perhaps if you knew him very well, your prediction would be better. Les smiled grimly. No man knew another that well.

In fact, he admitted silently, *no man knew himself well enough to predict his own reaction to an entirely unprecedented situation!*

Outside, the terrible earth-glow had become intense. It was expanding like a misshapen balloon. Wispy clouds of high-energy were fingering out into space, followed shortly by the main mass as it dispersed. It was ten times the original diameter now, and increasing rapidly.

"It will take days," said Blaine. "Of our accelerated 'time'. But you know the end-point."

Ackerman knew. The end-point of this was a blank space in the solar system and a gradual re-establishment of the energy-distribution of the solar system to make up for the missing mass-energy and attraction of the destroyed earth.

"What can I do?" he asked helplessly.

"How did they hit the earth?"

"I don't know," answered Ackerman.

"They had observers, just as we are. They got here by penetrating the no-world between the world-lines as we have done. We—you—must develop a means of our doing that. You, Ackerman, are really the only one in historic time who knows the secret of temperon."

"No, I do not."

Calvin Blaine smiled tolerantly. "I am of the destroyed earth," he said sadly. "We do not know how to penetrate the barrier."

"But you are here," said Les.

Blaine nodded very slowly. "Yes—because you, Les Ackerman, know that secret."

"But I don't—I don't!"

"You will recall it. You will work; you will succeed. And once you succeed in penetrating the secret of the barrier between the twin possibilities, you will help us. Then we will be able to come through into this temporal freedom of this unreal existence—to help you!"

Ackerman groaned. "I am the man," he said quizzically, "who travels backwards in 'time' to write himself a set of plans on how to build a 'time machine' which he is now using to deliver the letter."

"Indeed."

"And so," Laurie said, smiling, "you reach down, grasp yourself by the shoelaces, and lift."

"Ridiculous.... But I will help!"

Calvin Blaine caught Ackerman's hand in a firm grasp. Laurie pressed his other arm against her in a gesture of real affection. Ackerman felt, within him, the beginnings of a glow of success—

And at that precise moment the ship lurched, throwing them all off balance.

CHAPTER 5

Calvin Blaine cursed, strove to disentangle himself from Ackerman, who was trying to raise both his weight and that of Blaine from Laurie, who was pressed harshly across the heavy desk; its edge was cutting into her spine.

The lurch changed direction and hurled them all from the desk and across the tiny room against the wall. This time the combined weight of Laurie and Ackerman crushed Blaine to the wall, and drove the breath from him. He struggled weakly; Laurie slipped to the floor, gasping.

Ackerman, cushioned first by the girl and second by her father, was dizzy, but not harmed. Blaine slipped to the floor as Les Ackerman stooped and lifted the girl to her feet.

Then there was a metallic, grinding sound; shortly afterwards three men strode in and snapped handcuffs over the wrists of Laurie and Calvin Blaine.

"You're lucky," one of them said to Ackerman.

"Lucky?" snorted Ackerman. "That's what he told me when he met Tansie and me."

"You're luckier this time," laughed the leader. "I'm Barry Ford. The guy with the manacles and the policeman's mien is Tod Laplane. He who fondles the firearm is a trigger by the name of Louis Ford. He is fortunate enough to share the same parents with me."

Louis grinned cheerfully. "Sharing a fine set of parents has but one drawback," he told Ackerman. "It requires that I acknowledge Barry as my blood brother. It shouldn't happen to a salamander, let along a dog."

Barry smiled genially. "Well," he said, "you're luckier—and have always been in better company—than I am—and have been."

Laplane turned away from his handiwork. "Shall it be pistols and coffee at daybreak?" he laughed.

"Look," said Ackerman, interested in the horseplay but annoyed by the entire occurrence, "Suppose you jokers forget your unreal animosities and tell me what's going on."

"All's fair—" said Barry Ford.

"—In love and war," finished his brother Louis.

"Is that what this is?" demanded Ackerman.

"By and large," agreed Barry. "You've just witnessed the destruction of a world; their world," he added, pointing at Laurie and Calvin Blaine. "That, I must admit, was engineered by our world." To the latter word Barry added the gesture of pointing to his brother and the other man, Laplane.

"It was not a pretty sight," snapped Ackerman; "are you going to try to justify it?"

Blaine grunted angrily. "No one can justify wanton destruction.

"Remember, Ackerman, that what you have just observed is but a close probability. Believe this because we cannot prove it right now—we will later—but we have as interesting a scene to show you concerning our world. Engineered, I might say, by Blaine and his very lovely daughter."

"He told me that I was the man who could avert that affair."

"Uh-huh," grinned Barry wolfishly. "You are. You were well on the way to averting it. Look, Ackerman, how long do you think this unnatural splitting of the 'time-stream' can continue?"

"I don't know."

"Well, not much longer. This unreal 'time-space' comes to an end not far from here, Ackerman. The ending of 'time-space'—this unreal existance between two probabilities ends; and he who lets the normal passage of 'time' catch up with him is, at the end of this 'time-space', trapped in the natural world. That is the 'future' and will always be the 'future' to those of us who roam this 'time-space' in the hope of averting the tragedy. When we all have succeeded, we will all come to the end of 'time-space', here and not long hence, and permit ourselves to be caught up with the natural pattern of life. Your friends here—my enemies—were about to accomplish their purpose."

"Purpose?" said Ackerman trying to follow the other man's reasoning. "Is it a foul purpose to try to prevent the death of a world?"

Ford nodded. "You, Ackerman, are destined to save the situation. Blaine and Blaine, here, were about to permit you—with them—to be caught up with the ending of this 'time-space'. Then the brilliant Lester Ackerman would be lost to 'time-space' forever. The real tragedy would come, but the minor tragedy that only they consider worthy, would have been averted. So long as you remain in 'time-space', Ackerman, the destruction of their earth is a definite probability."

"Sounds like a good reason for leaving."

"Yes? Then listen: So long as you remain in 'time-space' the destruction of my world is improbable."

Calvin Blaine glared, and he spoke up. "Ackerman, what he says is true, in part; because he intends to use you to develop a means of destroying my world. If you pass into the future, our own scientists will succeed first and therefore be able to destroy his world."

"You're in the middle," said Laurie in a sympathetic voice. "No matter which you do, you've got the fate of a world on your head. I believe," she added wistfully, through welling eyes, "that I might have been able to make you forget that. In fact, had it been mine to say, you'd have been spared knowing that upon your shoulders lies the decision as to which existance should be saved. It is a question that no mortal should ever be called upon to decide."

"Come," said Barry Ford to Ackerman. He ignored the girl's plea. "We've got to get out and into our own ship. This one is drifting toward the end of 'time-space'; we'll be caught."

"Even now," said Laurie in a voice that wrenched Ackerman's heart, "I could ease the hurt; make you forget that such a problem once was yours. He'll leave us to drift, Les. We'll be caught and taken from this life. If you decide—please come. To—me?"

Barry turned roughly and snapped: "You'd sell yourself for your world?"

"It would not be a difficult sale," she answered.

"But a bargain hard to keep pure," he snorted.

Laurie smiled. "It often happens," she said with a ring of sincerity, "that duty and logic both direct one toward his heart's desire; that's when life is best."

"And you?" Barry scowled.

"I find neither duty nor logic to be odious terms," she said; "and I'm not one to abandon a pleasant idea just because it isn't original with me."

Louis Ford suddenly jumped. "Hurry!" he shouted. "She's stalled us to the danger point!"

"Trickstress," scorned Barry.

"They lie!" screamed Laurie. "Lester—believe me!"

Calvin Blaine turned to her. "Les will do as *he* believes," he said. "And all is not lost. We may yet win; remember—this, too, is but probability!"

Louis Ford and Tod Laplane grabbed Les Ackerman by the arms and hurried from the ship, into theirs. Les heard Laurie's fading voice crying through sobs for him to stay.

The door of the other ship rapped shut and cut off the cries. "A consummate actress," said Barry levelly.

Ackerman turned to him. "I presume that Tansie Lee is one of your crowd? Frankly, I really don't know who to believe."

Barry laughed shortly. "Tansie Lee? She is none of my crowd; she's a weak-minded sitter on the temporal fence, Ackerman. She believes that both worlds can be saved."

"Well, can't they?"

"Oh, now look, Ackerman, you're not the same kind of wishy-washy creature. Life is a struggle always. Kill or be killed still works—and always will."

"Just destruction for the sake of," said Ackerman harshly, "is untenable—even though you indulge in self-justification by believing that life is always kill or be killed."

"Let's face it," said Barry Ford. "Before your perilous experiment, we had a single world, with a single 'future'. You caused fission of 'time'. The twin existances are starting to converge again; the energy used in splitting 'time' is dissipating and as it is converted, the 'time-streams' converge. But they have not been the same world for hundreds of years. What will happen when suddenly the solar system contains two suns, two earths, and two of each planet? The sky will be filled with double stars where single stars once were, and quadruple stars where doubles now exist. Some, that have not moved far from one another in their contingent existances, will find one another occupying the same 'space'! See?"

Ackerman scowled uncertainly. "It looks to me as though we're scheduled for a big blast anyway."

Ford shook his head with a slight smile. "Nope," he said. "Not at all; you see, Ackerman, there is only one thing that tends to draw the coincident existances together. One force against the fissioning force of your little experiment. If we can destroy that force, the twin lives will continue to drift apart."

"And that force?"

"That force, Ackerman, is the physical energy of the human mind!"

"Uncontrolled? What is the affinity?"

Barry bit his lip and shrugged. "Human cussedness," he said. "Why, fundamentally, are you a brilliant physicist?"

"I'm not; and I've been called that by too many people."

"You are and we'll pursue the question. Why?"

Ackerman grinned. "Just apelike curiosity," he said. "I like to know what makes things tick."

"Research," said Barry, "revealed to our world that this 'time-split' did obtain. It was announced. Instantly all people began to wonder what the other one looked like, whether he had a 'time-brother' on the other one, and every man, woman, and child found himself hoping, someday, to join the other world. Doubtless those of the other earth did likewise."

Ackerman nodded absently. "You can destroy the earth but you can't change human nature, is that it?"

"With precision."

Ackerman thought for a moment. Then he said: "I'm in the middle; I've been told by three groups that within my mind lies the hope of salvation. That may be so, but where it lies I'll be unable to tell until someone tells me. Maybe I'll meet myself here in 'time-space'. Then perhaps I can tell me." He laughed bitterly.

"However," he said roughly, "I'm still in the middle. I've been led around both by the nose and by emotions and logic that may be correct—or sheer sophistry. Someone should haul off and tell me the truth, the whole truth, and nothing but; too many people seem to be keeping things to themselves. Like the gang who is afraid to vote for a square deal because a square deal means that they'd get what was coming to them and they know they wouldn't like what they deserved.

"Everyone seems more than willing to make use of me to further their own ends. I'm still in the middle because I don't know the whole story.

"However again," he said with a sour smile, "there is one item upon which all warring groups agree. And that, gentlemen, is that Lester Ackerman's mind contains the answer to the problem. Until I know what the answer is, I'm unable to help friend or foe, or in between. Nor," he added, "do I know which is which, yet.

"Therefore," he finished, "I'll go along with you because you happen to have captured the pawn in free gambit; perhaps I'll learn the answer to all of my questions at the same time."

Barry and Louis Ford and Tod Laplane listened quietly. Then Barry nodded. "You've been pulled this way and that way, Ackerman, because you were unable to move on your own; it is an admission of weakness to refuse the other side its due. It is an admission of strength, belief in one's own ideals, and faith in the rightness of himself if he is not only willing for the other side to be heard, but urges it. Well, Ackerman, we think we're right and we'll take you at your word; we have every reason to believe that our side of this complicated story is the soundest."

"Then how do I start?"

Barry smiled. "We all need a means of entering 'time-space' from a real existance; you are the only one able to do it so far."

"But you're here."

"We are—but excellent probabilities; we are proof that you succeeded. You might fail, Ackerman, and then our life would remain on our individual worlds. Our life here will fade and all we've been able to do will also disappear."

"And me?" asked Les, puzzling. "Am I a real identity, wandering through an unreal realm of fancy?"

"This is an unreal world," said Barry thoughtfully. "Therefore you must be unreal, too. However, if you fail, it will be as though you died in that explosion. If you succeed, you will live again. With us!"

CHAPTER 6

Barry Ford, unlike Les Ackerman's other companions, was set up for work. Tansie had wanted to show him first and explain afterwards; what her real purpose was, Les Ackerman could not divine. He suspected her motives deeply; after all, Tansie was a married woman by her own admission, a fact she had not mentioned until it had been forced from her. Not only that, but she had behaved like a woman who was not only interested in him but who also wanted his interest in her. Ackerman squirmed uncomfortably as he recalled his complete, doglike faith. He'd missed the ring; it was small and of natural gold that blended with Tansie's golden skin. He suspected that she had been careful to keep her left hand either out of sight or in motion, so that he could not see it.

The Blaines at least, were more straightforward; there was less mystery to them. Or, he admitted, their purpose had been uncovered by Barry Ford and Company. At least there seemed to be no perfidy there. Laurie was justified in trying to save her own earth. It was a rather involved question; one that might never be solved. Ackerman might never be sure whether Laurie's interest was real. Saving a world was a large item, one that might drive a person into most any devious act. He had no doubt that Laurie was a consummate actress, as Barry Ford claimed. Calvin Blaine was equally justified. Ackerman smiled grimly. He saw no reason to vote for one against the other; he did not subscribe to their policy, which was to save their own at whatever expense to any other, yet he was firm in his own willingness to admit that they were justified in their own minds. Placed in a similar position, Ackerman knew that he would lie, cheat, and steal to save his own earth from destruction.

But things were clearer. Ackerman held no illusions now. He pegged Barry Ford right. Ford, of course, was smart; he knew that by this time there could be little chance for blind leading. His sensible course was to admit the conflict and ask Ackerman to view both sides before acting. Also, grinned Ackerman, Barry Ford was smart enough to realize that after having two women hurled at him, Les would be inclined to view any other such acts as sheer folly. The adage said: Once burned, twice shy. After twice scorched, how skittish for the third time?

He had completed the circle of thought; he was back to Barry Ford. The third party in this wild game was, unlike the others, set up for laboratory investigation; Les admitted once that he did not know about Tansie Lee and the Blaines. Maybe they were also set up. He hadn't been around that long.

Les Ackerman was beginning to understand the basis for the famed General Semantics. It was fine to know what was "truth", or feasible, or "good". It was even better to know what was not "truth", or "good", or feasible; that implied a greater recognition of knowledge. Thomas Edison was reported to have known several thousand things about his nickel storage battery that would not work.

The trouble with Ackerman, he himself realized, was that he knew nothing at all. It was an insane program; he was here, aided and working for men who were able to get here because Les had been successful in his work. And then they blithely stated, coldly and calmly, that so soon as he proved himself unable to succeed, they would all disappear!

He shook his head, and then grinned. Fervently he prayed that this was not a wild dream; it was such a fearful mess that any waking would be a sorry anticlimax. He recalled Doctor Forbes, the eminent psychiatrist, who once said that there was absolutely no way to prove to one's own satisfaction that he was either dreaming or awake. He remembered that especially because he'd had a dream shortly afterwards in which he dreamed that he had just awakened from a dream. Doctor Forbes had nodded when told, had mentioned that his subconscious had used that method to try to prove to his dreaming mind that the dream was real.

He stopped thinking along those lines. That way madness lay. It was reminiscent of the childlike reasoning that asks: "But Daddy, who brings the baby storks?"

Or, he reconsidered irrelevantly, how many angels can stand on the point of a pin.

There was another, more pertinent thing. On that point, Ackerman left his room and went to Barry Ford. "Look, Barry," he said. "I want to know how *you* got here."

"You brought us through."

"And where is the equipment I used?"

Barry shook his head. "I don't know right now."

"And I suppose that the Blaines came likewise?"

Barry nodded.

Les Ackerman shook his head. "I've been shoved around so much, that I see little reason in bringing this gang through so that you can all shove me around. I'd like to go back myself."

"You can never go back," said Barry, sincerely. "And you'll find that living in this 'time-space' is not the bed of roses it might seem. It gets goddam lonesome. You'll get wild for the touch of an honest whim. We bring through only what we plan ahead for; you must plan every item, Ackerman, which leaves the chance-factor of living completely out. There is no getting up in the middle of the night to take a run to the corner drugstore for a cup of coffee. Or calling up your girl for a quick date as a pleasant surprise. If you hope to do something like that, you've got to plan it ahead and say to yourself: '*On the seventieth evening in 'time-space', I shall surprise my beloved by presenting her with—something very unperishable.*' I'm sorry that I cannot help you, Ackerman."

"You might have brought the equipment through with you."

"Or a model? No go, Ackerman; the thing isn't like a radio set or a small cyclotron. It's more a matter of force fields and energy gradients, as I too-vaguely understand it."

"Why didn't anybody think to ship through a physicist?"

Ford snapped the communicator on and called: "Fellows, come here, all of you!"

Louis Ford came first, and Tod Laplane. Then a striking brunette that Ackerman had not seen before—and for whom Barry said, quickly: "This is Tod's sister Joan; she's here as a general statistician and recorder, and not for the purpose of enticing you."

"That's not very complimentary to either of us," said Ackerman.

Joan smiled honestly. "No, it isn't. But it is true, Lester. You see, I'm a gatherer of facts; I know how people have been trying to use you. I promise—we will not."

Tod smiled at her and then asked: "Why the general call, Barry?"

Barry grinned. He gave them a brief resume of the talk and discussion, and Ackerman's questions of why it couldn't be done by copying the models used to bring them through. Then, with a flourish and a beautifully executed counterfeit of Lester Ackerman's voice, tone, and diction, said: "Why didn't anybody think to ship through a physicist?"

Laughter rang through the ship. Barry himself broke down and leaned weakly against the desk. Tod Laplane fell inert into a chair and shook with gales of silent laughter. Louis Ford merely gulped inanely, and Joan added her mirth in a gurgling contralto.

"Okay," snapped Ackerman, "so soon as I find the face I dropped here somewhere, I'll leave."

That stopped the laughter. "Look, Ackerman, *you're* the great physicist; why should we have another?"

Ackerman snorted. "The next character who calls me a 'great physicist' either with or without capital letters is going to get a mouthful of fist," he snarled; "I'm tired of being the main point in a joke."

Barry sobered quickly. "It is not used in a sense of ridicule or insult."

"I don't give a damn how it is used. I don't like a lot of people calling me a veritable messiah. I'd not like it even if their tongues weren't shoved eight miles out in their cheeks. So stop it, unless you'd like to go a few swift ones with me."

Barry nodded. "Sorry, Ackerman. But—you understand—we know you brought us here. Within your own mind and your own ability, you have the secret to the big question."

"About all I know about the physics of this business is that it started with a few grams of temperon."

"We'll get you some temperon," said Barry. "And a cyclotron. And most anything else you're likely to need."

"Good," snorted Ackerman. "Get me a lie detector; eight gallons of scopolamine and a psychiatrist—and have 'em comb my mind. Frankly, I'd like to know the answer, too."

Ackerman settled for the cyclotron and the temperon. He spent a week of trying, but little came of it, according to him. Barry Ford had come well prepared. The mass spectrograph was a beaut; the cyclotron was a physicist's dream; and the physico-chemical laboratory must have set someone back a cold half billion.

And to top it all, Ackerman had been the mainspring that brought it through, and was now trying to figure out how and why.

He learned more about the nuclear properties of temperon. They were nothing to get excited about, or he considered them normal until the statistician-girl, Joan Laplane looked up from her notes and asked, innocently: "Temperon is stable. The neutron-isotope—making it the next atom-number above, is radioactive. But I note that it is doubly radioactive."

"It is. It either emits an alpha particle and drops two numbers and four masses down, or emits a beta ray and jumps a number up with no change in mass. In the first case the resultant is stable. In the second case, the resultant then emits an alpha particle and an electron and becomes stable—the same element."

"But why should it emit one of two particles?"

"That's a normal state for many radioactives," said Ackerman. "Radioactivity is a sign of atomic instability. The ejection of the unbalancing particle is not instantaneous. It takes 'time'. In the meantime, the nucleus is unbalanced. Now, this unbalance energy is distributed among the particles of the nucleus, and depending whether the alpha collects the necessary energy first or whether the random rambling of this energy drives out a beta ray, we have the splitting of the radioactive ladder. It happens, for instance, in all three of the normal radioactive chains: Thorium, actinium, and uranium. Thorium drops down the scale normally, dropping alpha particles and beta rays until it reaches Thorium C, which is an isotope of bismuth—bismuth 212. There it splits into Thorium C' or Thorium C". Thorium C' emits alpha and becomes lead 208; Thorium C" emits a beta ray and—likewise—becomes lead 208."

"Might it mean an unknown structure of the nucleus?" she asked.

"Might," he said reflectively. "There's isotopes—elements with the same atomic number but different masses. There's isobars—elements with the same atomic masses but different numbers. Maybe there's you-name-it-*bars* with similar masses and numbers but different structures."

"Different meson activity."

"Mesobars?" he laughed; "I'll buy that." It intrigued him, and he went on: "Maybe temperon, in splitting into two different possible atoms produces a situation whereby the reactions between the two elements results in something new in nuclear physics."

Barry Ford looked up and said: "I could see that it might be messy if Element X fissioned into radioiodine and radiophosphorus."

"Not phenomenally so," replied Ackerman, shaking his head. "A few atoms of explosive chemical mixture is still small peanuts to the energy of a radioisotope, let along a true fission. And the resulting chemical combination still has the radio-isotopes in it which will emit and change. Chemical combination of an atom of hydrocarbon and oxygen produces a few electron volts. Alpha from any radioisotope runs into millions of electron volts."

"Um. Well, what have you got?"

"I don't know," said Ackerman; "I've got to think."

He stood up and stretched, and said he was going for a walk. Idly, he hefted the bombarded temperon on his fingers and then dropped it into a side pocket. He turned and left the laboratory.

It was on earth, of course, set in the backhills of Wisconsin, several miles from Ladysmith. Ackerman wanted to roam the roadways, and possibly gaze upon one of the handy lakes and wish fervently that he was not trapped in a no-world where he could do nothing but fume.

A car came up behind him, and he stopped to watch. It was not a phantom car of the real world, but a 'time-space' car of his unreal existance. Joan Laplane leaned out. "Ride," she stated; "gets farther and leaves energy to enjoy whatever you're seeking."

"Okay," he said. "What I want to do, I guess, is to ride through a city and watch people."

"That's masochism," she told him.

"Perhaps," he nodded. "But it's also a matter of frustration; I'll ride if you'll drive this hickey through traffic."

"Right through," she said with a cheerful laugh.

It was rather hair-raising, to Les. The girl drove well, but downright recklessly. That is, until he remembered that they could drive through any other car in motion.

Joan Laplane drove through other cars to pass them, and at one time she enjoyed driving on the left side of the road through a careening coupe that was racing towards them. It gave Ackerman a thrill and, in a sense, helped him to relax.

Then they were in the town of Ladysmith, a minute metropolis of about ten thousand people, but large enough in relation to the other towns in the vicinity to be the county seat. Joan brazenly selected a fine parking place in between two *No Parking* signs in front of the city hall, and backed her car through the cars of two of the local politicians who were nepotically disregarding the signs.

"That'll show 'em," she said with a grin.

"Why stop?"

"I want to dance," she told him. "We'll not pay entry, nor can we buy a drink. But we can use their floor and we can dance right through the other customers and never get an elbow in the ribs."

Ackerman laughed. This 'time-space' had some advantages. "But if your feet get trampled, I can't blame some clumsy-footed stranger."

Joan nodded, and her raven hair rippled tantalizingly. "Nope," she said, "you can't; so if you dance on my feet I'll bark your shin with a spike heel. Fair enough?"

"Fair," he said.

CHAPTER 7

With smiles of mutual amusement, Joan and Les walked through the door of a small nightclub, past the hatcheck girl, past the headwaiter, and into the clubroom. "First time," said Joan, "that anybody has ever got into a jernt like this without paying well for the privilege."

"It has its disadvantages," said Ackerman; "we get no table."

"That's easy," laughed Joan. She led Les across the dancefloor and seated herself on the edge of the bandstand, sitting right through the saxophone player's music stand. Ackerman sat beside her, his shoulder partway through the cornetist's knee. It was sometime later that they both noticed that they were not really sitting on the bandstand but upon something as firm at least three inches below the floor-level. It was, he was beginning to understand, a matter of temporal mass and temporal inertia—which Ackerman associated with permanence, dependability, and ponderosity. The earth was quite permanent; it had been a functioning factor for a good many billion years. The building was more or less permanent, but far from having the permanence of a brick wall, for instance.

The music started and they danced; it was fun even though their feet moved ankle deep in the floor. The floor, of course, was polished and waxed. They were dancing on something that was less slick, but the matter of dancing in itself was enjoyable enough to reduce all discomfort to a minimum.

"I'd still like to order a drink," said Ackerman.

Joan shook her head. "I haven't a flask," she told him. Her statement was unnecessary. Her grandmother might have been able to conceal several quarts in and among the voluminosity of clothing. Joan Laplane, like most of the other girls of her day, would have been baffled to conceal a fluid ounce unless internally.

Liquor was not really necessary; Ackerman enjoyed himself. Joan was an excellent dancer and she was willingly lissome in his arms. She attracted him, and he was rapt in the enjoyment of the moment; so rapt that he noticed but gave no thought to the tickling movement against his hip.

It was neither annoying nor pleasant; it was easily ignored. Whatever it might be, it could wait.

But as they moved across the phantom dancefloor, the tickling motion increased slowly, raising its violence by degrees until it was no longer something to be put aside.

Ackerman gave it thought, then. It was, as he had subconsciously known all along, the sample of temperon. It was, inexplicably, moving.

Ackerman watched it carefully, after that. He said nothing. Luckily, Joan Laplane was the kind of girl who dances silently, enjoying the silent communion of musical and physical pleasure. Therefore she did not notice that Lester's attention was directed more toward something else. Ackerman was glad that his dancing was good enough to perform without complete attention, otherwise he would not be able to keep his secret.

It—increased.

He noted it, smiled, and deliberately steered Joan and himself through another dancing couple. It was one way to make the desired test—to prove what he was beginning to suspect.

It had the desired result, but the aftermath was astounding.

The girl of the couple through which Ackerman had passed suddenly squirmed, stopped dancing. Ackerman steered Joan four quick steps away and made a graceful but swift turn so that he could look over her shoulder.

The other girl turned, took a quick bead on the man dancing behind her, and let him have the flat of her hand across his face.

At that instant, the music died in a cacophony and the chattering of the crowd died with it.

"Get fresh!" snapped the girl.

"What did I do?" asked the dumfounded man, rubbing his face.

The girl let him have her other hand on the other side of his face. "That'll tell you!" screamed the girl in a voice that would have awed Medusa the Gorgon.

Her escort, puzzled, stepped forward between the other two. "What's going on?"

"I don't know," answered the slapped one; "all of a sudden she ups and cracks me."

"Must've been a reason," snarled the man. "Out with it!"

The slapped-one's girl friend faced the insulted girl. "Free with your hands, aren't you, dearie?"

"So's he!" she snapped in return.

"So'm I!" screeched the other girl. She reached and came back with a handful of hair. The other girl raked four red furrows down the side of the hair-puller's cheek, and the battle was on.

"Get her out!" snapped the slapped man.

"G'wan," snarled the other fellow; he led with a right, crossed with a left, and was jolted with a short jab to the stomach.

That was the end. Waiters, bouncers, and general huskies converged. The orchestra leader rapped and the band started to play a Spike Jones arrangement of *After the Brawl was Over!*

"Wisconsin," chuckled Les, "Seems to offer everything!"

To Joan, the sentimental spell was broken: Ackerman sensed this, and took her by the arm, leading her towards the door. She went, chuckling over the incident. It was Ackerman who was slightly horrified; he knew that he had been the cause of the ruckus. He was also pleased at the results, and he believed that he might be able to do something with this strange element.

He found passing through the door slightly difficult. The temperon sample in his pocket was slowed, as though a slight resistance were offered. The outer door moved slightly as he passed through it.

Joan, unknowing, drove home in the same reckless fashion. Ackerman prayed that they would meet no more careening cars; he was afraid that he might lose the sample if it caught in a swiftly moving body. This time, luck was with him.

Les Ackerman viewed his handiwork a week later. "'Tis a real monkey-motion," he told himself, "but it should work."

It was a real Rube Goldberg, of the type often concocted for an especial test. Many kinds may be seen in any laboratory, working madly to life-test various operating members, dropping parts against steel plates to see how many bumps they will take before becoming useless.

This was similar, but adapted to a singular purpose.

It was a straight reciprocating motion that passed an arm containing the sample of temperon back and forth through the trunk of a tree. The tree, of course, was in 'Real Time'; the machine in the 'time-space'. It would have simplified things if the treetrunk could be fastened to, but it was not; so the amount of drag was measured by the forces—back-forces—that tended to resist the motor that drove the gadget. At the end of each stroke, the arm entered a chamber that carried a radioactivity counter.

The tree was five or six miles from the laboratory, and only Ackerman knew where it was.

Ackerman, having been twice bitten, was thrice shy times ten. At this point, his own mother might have had trouble in convincing Ackerman that she meant only for his benefit.

At the end of another week, Ackerman was satisfied; he was certain. For the drag versus 'time' had passed through a wide peak. The radioactivity versus 'time' had been harder to unravel, for it possessed an irregular curve that Ackerman fought with for hours before it resolved sensibly into the superposition of several normal radioactivity curves.

The matching of the drag curve with one of the radio curves was simple, after that. And Les then spent another ten days figuring out which of the many resulting radio-isotopes of temperon was responsible for its extension through the barrier of time into the world of 'Real Existance'.

His progress after that was rapid. Barry, Louis, Tod and Joan were baffled by his actions and said so. They did see progress, and were pleased.

But they could offer no help. What Les was doing with the temperon sample was enigmatic to them, though he admitted that what they saw might lead them to the right answer eventually. A savage, given the knowledge only of the identification of materials and the working model, could easily reproduce a simple radio receiving set, yet he would have no idea as to the principles underlying the art. And many millions of people drive automobiles daily without the vaguest idea of the theory of the internal combustion engine.

The gloves that Ackerman made, studded with thin slices of temperon, enabled him to move and handle objects in the world of reality. Then the machine—with its huge paraboloidal reflector coated on the inside with a thin layer of temperon—gave Lester Ackerman his initial taste of success.

Out in the forest, far from the laboratory, Ackerman focused the reflector on a log, lying ghostlike in the world of 'Real Time'. It came through. Not as an object might be passed or drawn through a curtain to drop on the inside, or as an object lifted from a pool of water, passing from one medium to the other. It merely solidified.

He picked it up, grunting with the effort, and passed one end through a tree. Satisfied, he dropped it from his shoulder.

He turned—and then turned again, startled. His ears perked, and the sound came again.

Looking through the trees—it was like trying to see through a heavy maze of plate glass, and the scene fifty yards from him was as hidden as if the woods had been truly solid.

"Don't be alarmed," said a voice. Ackerman straightened.

"Spying?"

"You've been successful, we see," replied Barry Ford, ignoring his accusation.

"So?" demanded Ackerman.

"I might point out that you happen to be working for us."

"Interesting. I have other ideas," returned Ackerman testily. "Since I happen to be responsible for all of you, I happen to think that I have the right to do as I damn well please."

While speaking, Ackerman had been remembering that he had no freedom. He would have preferred to work alone. And if this decision was to rest as it seemed upon him, he should be permitted to make his decision unaided—or untrammelled. The idea of trying to select which one of two worlds had a better right to the future was no problem to ponder while being badgered.

Furthermore, this outfit had little more to offer than the Blaines.

Ackerman nodded inwardly, then turned the projector and snapped the reversing switch.

Barry leaped forward. His brother Louis shouted angrily. Tod Laplane lifted his gun, and Joan cried out in alarm. Tod Laplane fired, aiming for the heart of Ackerman's projector.

The bullet—passed through.

Then the Laplane-Ford faction, wraithlike already, faded from view, leaving Ackerman alone.

Alone? Not quite. Ackerman had another watcher, who now came into view. "Very interesting," said Calvin Blaine. "But I fear that you have done that which will cause the destruction of my world, young man."

"How?" demanded Ackerman. "And I thought that you and Laurie were trapped at the edge of time-space."

"You know my daughter?" asked Calvin Blaine in surprise. He called out, and Laurie came into view. "He knows you," said Calvin.

"Who is he. Is he Lester Ackerman?"

Ackerman put hands on hips and stared. "I am Les Ackerman," he said; "and this is beyond me."

"It is beyond me, too," said Calvin. "However, the destruction of my world is not a pleasant contemplation, Ackerman."

"I know; I've seen it."

"You have?"

"Yes," said Ackerman. "You showed it to me."

"No such thing," replied Laurie. "But we will, if you like."

Ackerman began to catch on. "You may, eventually," he said with a cryptic grin. "But tell me, how is my sending them back into their own world going to be instrumental in destroying yours?"

"Theirs is the world of free research," said Blaine. "Up to now, they know little of the true state of affairs, but once they return with the information, there will be trouble."

"I gather that if I'd kept them here, the initial knowledge would never reach that world?"

"You aren't properly acquainted with the chronological factors involved with the conservation of matter and energy," said Blaine. "When you sent them back, you sent them back to the precise instant of their leaving. In that way and in that way alone can the 'Real Time' constancy be preserved. This 'time-space' state is unreal, and therefore most anything can happen here. But they will return complete with all the knowledge they need to start the destruction of my world."

"Then," said Ackerman, "I shall stop them."

"You have 'time'," said Blaine. "But first, tell me how you happen to know of us."

Ackerman explained his actions up to the point of his meeting with Tansie. At that point, both Blaines exploded: "Tansie Lee!"

"Know her?" asked Ackerman quietly.

"She is a rather headstrong woman," said Blaine. "Full of a rather pale, idealistic plan to save both worlds with danger to none."

Laurie eyed Ackerman with interest. "You know her?"

Ackerman nodded glumly.

"Interesting," replied Laurie. "Imagine a real man who knows Tansie Lee without becoming captivated by her rather lush charm."

"I don't go in for running around with married women," said Ackerman.

"You're not married?"

"No," he said.

Calvin interrupted what was getting uncomfortable to Ackerman. "What happened then?" he asked. Les explained the rest, but omitted the minute details of his interrupted love-scene. He did tell them—by way of explanation—that his being in the company of Tansie Lee was due to the fact that he did not know she was married.

"I'm beginning to understand," said Blaine.

Ackerman nodded. "Go ahead," he said. "But be careful."

Laurie looked puzzled. "I don't get it."

Calvin turned to his daughter. "We've got to hurry," he said; "we've got to meet Lester Ackerman and Tansie Lee, take Ackerman to the edge of time to see the destruction of our world."

"Then it is to be destroyed?" said Laurie fearfully.

"It is only an excellent probability," said her father. "That may—it please God—be averted. Come."

CHAPTER 8

Ackerman ran to the laboratory and climbed into another 'time-vehicle'. He drove it through "time" and "space" as fast as he could, returning to the forest area where he had sent the group back. Once there, he pursued a blind train forward in "time", hurrying to catch them.

Swiftly he moved, but as fast as he was, they were always lost ahead of him. In effect, their return was instantaneous, but so was his flight across the years. It was only to Ackerman that "time" seemed to hang heavily as he drove futureward, stopping at regular intervals to see through the gray haze that covered up the outside when the vehicle was in motion.

At long last he saw them, but only for an instant and then through a fading fog.

Again he saw them, hurried ahead of them and waited. They re-appeared in the same postures of their leaving, were present for a bare instant, and then were gone again.

There were houses there the next "time", houses and people that got in his way; the next "time" again, there was a village, and then a small city was there.

But the returning group were slowing, and Ackerman saw that they were changing their posture a bit. The looks of anger and fear were dying; tenseness was leaving their bodies; they were turning to face one another.

It was upon the next "time" that Ackerman snapped his projector at them. He might as well have snapped his fingers; nothing happened.

He wondered, then smiled in frustration. How could he bring an object in from the other world that was not there? He could not; he could but wait until they returned and then grab them quick, again, before they had a chance to do any damage.

He raced forward quite a distance and looked them over. They were moving now; walking and talking to one another. Ackerman could not hear them for he was in his "time-ship" with the "lid" down for instant flight. He cursed the haze; it made a careful estimate of the instant of their arrival almost impossible. Especially now when they were beginning to blend in with the people of the "real world."

He saw it, then. They were idly walking, coming on the "time-strata" of solidity a full yard above the ground. Descending; walking through a "Real World" building toward a "Real World" sidewalk. They would meet— their "Real World" identities who were coming along the street in the same formation, talking in the same fashion.

Converging, wraith and ghost came together, passed through one another, approached a perfect register. Then as they blended into one being each, Ackerman gave a sharp cry and slammed down on his switch.

He saw it again. They parted, wraiths from ghosts, and continued on their respective paths. The group in the "Real World" continued along the street, talking animatedly. The others—solid to Ackerman and themselves, stopped in baffled amazement.

They saw his car, and him. "What is this?" demanded Barry Ford. "Where did you come from? And how in the name of the Seven Deadly Sins do we seem to be walking—wading, so help me—ankle deep in the ground?"

Ackerman sat down in utter weariness. He had done it, all right. He had brought them! He had split the instant on the instant, and with this result.

In the world of "Reality", Barry and Louis Ford, and Joan and Tod Laplane were free to go and tell all. In his world of "time-space", Les Ackerman had four completely baffled people who would never have known of "time-space" and the split worlds if he, Ackerman, had not interfered.

He had wondered about the destruction of Calvin Blaine's world, had sent Blaine off to find his—Ackerman's—own previous "time-self" because it had been Ackerman's opinion that the destruction of Calvin Blaine's world only obtained in a situation where the Laplane-Ford group had been returned. That, he believed, was a transitory situation that would be averted as soon as he caught up with them.

Then came the next blaze of mental lightning. Calvin Blaine was no man's fool: knowing that Ackerman must release the other group after meeting Calvin for the first time, Blaine would also know that when he interrupted the love-scene, it would be Ackerman's first knowledge of Calvin Blaine.

Then. Right then. If Calvin and Laurie Blaine permitted themselves to be caught up with the so-called "edge of time-space" with Lester Ackerman, the latter would never meet the Laplane-Ford group.

There would be no telling no information, and hence no strife. That of itself would be fine. But the twin worlds would eventually come together, both in "space" and in "time", and trouble would ensue from that alone. He, Ackerman, was the only man who could do something about that.

Quickly, he brought the group before him up to date. He told them as much as he could, told them to go and meet the Blaines, who were trying to get lost through the edge of the "time-split". It took some telling, some explanation, and quite a bit of convincing.

Eventually, they agreed. "But how will we go?" asked Barry Ford.

Ackerman wondered, and then grinned. "Simple; I'll not wait long. For I shall send the next person I meet in 'time' to this instant to meet me. In fact," he said with genuine amusement, "I may send myself. And here I come now—see?"

The other car was sliding down, solidifying rapidly as it came into the "time-space" instant of Ackerman's Unreal "present".

"We—"

"Get going," said Les; "I want to talk to myself in peace and quiet." They left, and Ackerman went to the other car, which had landed.

The driver was a stranger. He was about Ackerman's size and build; perhaps a little less gaunt and strained. He had a certain grim humor; sardonic, but still compassionate.

He stepped from the car and faced Ackerman. "So," he said with a sarcastic leer, "You are Lester Ackerman. The Great Physicist!"

"Now listen," snarled Ackerman angrily. "I don't—"

"Well, well!" laughed the other. "Look, Ackerman; for a Great Physicist, you are certainly making a sheer mess out of this."

"It's pretty much of a mess as it is!"

"Only what you've made it. You know, I should really let you stew in your own juice; it'll make a better man of you. It's only that I want to see you come through this at all that I interfere. Chum, you've boiled up a real tangle."

"*I* have?"

"This mess is of your making," insisted the stranger. "Shall I recount?"

"Please do," snapped Ackerman superciliously. "But after you tell me who you are."

"I happen to be Tansie Lee's husband."

"You—" stammered Ackerman. That, possibly, was the one thing that could—and did—fluster him completely. Not only that, but he showed it in every line of his body, every gesture, every stammering syllable. The other got a laugh out of Ackerman's complete loss of personal control.

"Don't apologize," he said. "I sent Tansie Lee; I hoped that you would be smart enough to figure it out with her help. You aren't."

"Did you instruct Tansie Lee to make love to me?"

"Tansie did nothing wrong," said the man. "What was wrong— completely, and totally—was your attitude."

Then he held up a hand as Ackerman was about to continue. "Not now," he said. "You've got to untangle this mess first."

"Go ahead," said Les. "Untangle."

"You," said Tansie Lee's husband, "were met by my wife in a state of ignorance concerning this fine mixup. You were intercepted by the Blaines, whom you, yourself, sent recently to do the intercepting. You even gave them the information that would best cause the breakup of intelligent understanding between Tansie and yourself. The Blaines reached you and intercepted. That fouled up my initial plans. Then you and the Blaines were intercepted again by the Laplane-Ford outfit—which you again sent to do the intercepting. Interestingly snarled, Ackerman; but when Barry Ford told you with such certainty that the Blaines were leading you to the instant of entrapped no-return at the so-called 'edge of time-space', Barry Ford was merely echoing your own fears. Fears which were installed in you, by the way, by Barry, who was recounting your own—oh Hell and Damnation!"

"Mind telling me where the Blaines come in?"

"Certainly. But I won't. You brought them."

"I'll be damned if I bring them."

The other man smiled knowingly. "As you tried to corral the other gang?"

"Meaning?" demanded Les.

"There's many's the slip. '*A would some power the giftie gi'e us, to see ourselves as ithers see us,*'" quoted Tansie Lee's husband. "I suppose you're not to blame; but you will agree that it is quite a mess."

"Agreed. Now what do I do about it?"

"Ackerman, what started all this?"

"A strange explosion brought about by the temperon metal in the cyclotron-set-up."

"And how is it to end?"

Ackerman sat down and put his face in his hands. "I don't know," he said soberly. "It seems that I am to make a choice between worlds. I can save one but not the other."

As Ackerman sat there, face lowered and spirits lower, he was in complete misery and totally oblivious to everything about him. One thing only penetrated the depth of his introversion.

That one thing was the cool touch of a soft hand on his shoulder. There was a delicate scent—one that brought memories, both delicately fond and angrily disconcerting. Tansie Lee seated herself beside him and put an arm over his shoulder. "Don't do that to him," she said, speaking to her husband with pleading.

"I can't live his life," he answered; "one more thing, and he'll be all right."

Ackerman looked from one to the other, puzzled. Had he been the other man, he would have been consumed with jealousy. "What?" he asked weakly.

"I can't tell you completely," said the other, "but it has to do with the 'time-fission' and the temperon; you'll figure it out."

There came to Ackerman that he did have the answer. The way to solve the problem was to use his ability to remove the temperon from the cyclotron, and thus avert the explosion!

Tansie stood up. "Come on, Les," she said to him.

"Come on?" he asked dully.

"Yes," said her husband. "Finish what you started; you see, both Tansie and I have a rather large stake in this thing."

He turned and headed across the ground to a second time-ship, entered, and left.

Ackerman stood up and shook his head nervously. "Well, Mrs. Lee," he said, and he mentally winced as he used her pet prefacing word.

She smiled, gaminlike, and said: "But I'm not Mrs. Lee. Tansie Lee is my given name. You see, Les, I am Mrs. Lester Ackerman!"

"Ye—but—uh—"

She laughed gurglingly. "That's another thing that is completely wrong with this 'time-space'," she said; "right now I'm married to you but you aren't married to me. So if there's any question of convention, Lester, you are the guilty party, not I."

Ackerman sat back down again and groaned.

"But you be a good, sensible boy," she promised coyly, "And someday you will be."

"So that was—-me?" he asked in a strained voice.

She nodded.

"You mean to tell me that I didn't recognize myself?" he demanded.

Again she nodded. "You see, Les, you—and everybody—is used to seeing himself in a mirror. No face or person is symmetrical; that mole on your right cheek is always on your mirror image's left cheek—but it was still on the other Ackerman's right cheek. Also, you expected that if that ship did contain yourself, coming to get you as you so happily told the Ford-Laplane outfit, you expected that you would make some wisecrack about it. Therefore you didn't expect yourself to be coming as you did. Quite simple, I call it."

"Another angle on this mad tangle," said Les. "I'll be glad to get out of it."

"So will I," said Tansie.

"And I'm going to start right now!"

CHAPTER 9

Below them lay the depressed green-glaze bowl of atomic horror; above stood the silent laboratory, deserted and awaiting the arrival of the technicians for the next morning's work.

Hazily in sight was the temperon sample, and the radiation counters were clicking off at a fast rate.

"What are you going to do?" asked Tansie, in a voice that was filled with fear.

Ackerman stood up and stretched. "I am going to remove that sample," he said with an air of finality. "Then the time-fission will not take place, and there need be no ultimate conflict between the twin worlds."

"You mustn't," she breathed.

"No?"

"No," she told him. "For if you do, you shall not live. And we will never—" she let the sentence die.

He faced her squarely. "Tansie," he said, "It will be very easy for me to fall deeply in love with you. Given another day, and it would certainly obtain. Yet the lives and desires of two people must not prevail to the death and destruction of a world full of people. Though it mean death to me, I could not live knowing that billions of people died because I was selfish."

Tansie looked at him tearfully. "You'd sacrifice me?"

"You make it difficult," he said. "One life for a billion lives. And yet," he said, brightly, "you do exist; does that not prove something?"

"Only that in this world of probability and unreal existance, I am a definite probability."

"Yes," he told her. "This is the world of probability. I am not in the Real World, nor are you. If I do this, who is to tell me that we two may not go on forever in our own world of probability?"

"No," she said pleadingly. "Oh Les—I do so want—"

"I'll chance it," he said. "Because I must. I—look!"

Tansie turned. There, appearing with that thickening of the substance that characterized the arrival of a "time car" was the Blaines' ship. And beside it was the other one. Doors emerged, and the six got out of their ships and faced one another.

"So!" snapped Calvin Blaine. "We can finish this right here."

"Don't ask for mercy," snapped Barry Ford. "Nor expect sportsmanship. This is for keeps, and for the permanent existance of a whole world."

Tansie shuddered. "They'll fight," she said. "Because whichever side wins, they will prevent the others from returning to their worlds with the information that is needed. One and one alone will survive—and it is not fair, four to two, and Calvin Blaine an elderly man."

Tod Laplane lifted his gun; Laurie Blaine, her blonde hair a shining halo, pointed a revolver at Joan Laplane, who raced forward like a raven-haired fury, a gleaming knife in her hand. Barry Ford shook his broad shoulders and leaped—just as a shot rang out from the side.

They all turned. And across the space behind the Ford-Laplane ship there came another couple. A second Calvin and Laurie Blaine, armed.

In all, only four shots were fired before the embattled ones came to contact blows. Then the guns were wrested from fighting hands and it was tooth and nail.

"Come on," said Ackerman. "Because what you see is but eight people. If we do not, there will be that many billions of people fighting to the death."

Their motion caught eyes in the fighting crowd. Both sides were apparently wary of more re-inforcements. None of them knew how many would be coming back; it is conceivable that whole armies could be built up of people returning to fight this battle.

But it was Les and Tansie Lee that they saw, and they stopped. Then Les and Tansie were in their ship, and Les was at the control board.

The other crowd boiled in, behind them, the fight forgotten, momentarily. They wanted Les Ackerman above all, for he was in a position to nullify any of their acts, regardless of which side won. He was not going to elude them again; they would continue this battle in Ackerman's presence so that the winner would be able to overpower the physicist.

Ackerman nudged the automatic controls. The "time-space" vehicle started forward in space and backwards in "time".

Behind him the two factions eyed one another suspiciously, and moved warily to get into fighting-position.

Les turned briefly, and shook his head. Getting into that battle himself would be no good. *Let them fight!* he said to himself. *Give me "time".* Ackerman could best win by removing the cause.

He flipped the top-hatch open and groped out of the moving ship with his gloved hand—the temperon-coated glove—hoping to locate by sheer luck the cyclotron target and the temperon sample. By luck aided with a good memory of where it was. He thought for a moment that he, himself, was not far from here in both "time" and "space". He was separated in space by the radiation-proof barrier, and in "time" only by the few instants of temporal fission.

Then he saw it! Vaguely, dimly, distorted by the gray-green haze that enveloped the ship in motion.

The ship stalled. It could not penetrate the barrier of "time" to head into the "past" which would have been previous to the fission of "time". So Ackerman nudged the power up higher and the temporal drive of the ship strained against the barrier like an automobile straining against an immobile wall.

Ackerman reached for the temperon.

Tansie cried: "No, Les!" She ran to take his hands from the open hatch.

He took her by the shoulders and shook her gently. "You'll be all right," he said softly; "it is a chance we must take!"

"But—" she said uncertainly, and stopped because of the roar that came from behind.

"Ackerman!" bellowed Tod Laplane. "He's removing the original temperon!"

"If he does!" swore Barry Ford, "We'll not exist!"

Their private fight forgotten, both factions turned and hurled themselves at Ackerman.

Eight people to one—and Tansie Lee still against his purpose to boot; he shook her free and reached, missed and tried again.

The roar of noise stopped. Ackerman caught it out of the corner of one eye. Tansie Lee still believed that the removal of the temperon and the resulting correction of the "time-split" would make her non-existant, but she was standing there with a wicked-looking shotgun poised across one shapely hip. If she fired, the kick would turn her around, and Tansie knew it, for she was pointing the gun to her left. The second shot would sweep the right side of the room, and the chances were excellent that no one would be much alive after the third.

Limbo—the land of non-existance—might be her lot, but until she left here, no one was going to harm Les Ackerman.

He shook all thoughts from his mind and reached again. And this time he touched it!

The gray-green haze parted in a flare of light. Ackerman saw both the deuterium-ice target and the temperon clearly; it was the latter that gave him pause.

For out from the temperon sample was growing a shimmering, uncertain sphere of energy. It expanded and then hurled itself outward with lightning rapidity. Out it went, to the ends of the infinite universe.

Then destruction, sheer and complete, broke loose. The "time-ship" was hurled away, but not before they saw solid matter burst into a coruscation of incandescent gas, and flame up out of its wraithlike self into a pillar of boiling clouds that headed for the stratosphere. Below them, the ground seared upwards and sintered downwards and fused into an ugly gray-green glaze.

"So," said Ackerman, shaking with reaction. "So Lester Ackerman himself is the cause of the fission in 'time'. You may stop fighting, gentlemen. Tansie, you can stop pointing that cannon at them, too."

Calvin Blaine came forward and took it from her shaking hands. She turned blindly, like an automaton; then she looked up at Les and reality came once more across her face. "Les!" she cried and hurled herself forward into his arms.

Calvin turned to his other, "time-separated" self. "Please leave," he said. "This is most disconcerting."

One Laurie Blaine shrugged at the other. "I don't even like myself as competition," she said.

One pair of Blaines left the ship; the other Calvin Blaine looked out of the window and chuckled. "They left," he said, "just in time to get into that fight!"

"Then this," replied his daughter, "is the ship they came in."

"Ours is over there," said Blaine; "let's go."

"But what about them—and him?" asked Laurie indicating the others in Ackerman's ship.

"I think," said Blaine, "that nothing we do can change much right now; Ackerman himself is the one that must be moving next."

Barry Ford grunted angrily. It was quite apparent that a sudden thought had occurred to him. He herded his friends out and into their own ship.

"Hell!" said Blaine, taking Laurie by the arm and almost hurling her out.

"What's got into them?" asked Tansie.

"It has occurred to them that there is one more very definite danger for them all. They've got to go there to prevent it. Foolishly, they're hurrying when they know that I've got a lot of work to do first, and still will end up where they are at the proper instant."

"Work?" asked Tansie.

"Uh-huh," he said. "I've some correcting to do. Will you drive us along the Blaines' side of this 'Time-stream'. I'm going to peck at the typewriter a bit."

It was a long time later. Ackerman had written several thousand words on the subject, and was now peering through one of the ship windows at the laboratory through which the "time-space" ship was parked. Then, satisfied, he nodded. "Push here," he said cryptically.

"Huh?" asked Tansie.

"Part of my corrective work," he said. "So help me, I started this mess; I'm going to be the one that cleans it up."

He used the projector to drag a few odd items into the "time-space" from the "real world" laboratory.

"On the other side of that barrier," he told Tansie, "there are a couple of characters bootlegging a bit of private research."

"What are you going to do?"

"They are going to have themselves a high-grade atomic explosion."

"Won't that be dangerous? And how will it cause corrective measures?"

Les grinned with self-satisfaction. "This," he said waving his hands, "is the world of throttled research. Like all times of prohibition, there are people who will bootleg, whether it be liquor, dope, or knowledge. This explosion, however, will do two things to that world. They will understand that there are a lot of people doing the same thing—and will also know that this same thing might happen again and again, because no one has the faintest idea of what anybody else is doing! When the first chemist mixed gunpowder, he was able to warn other chemists not to mix more than so much—or else. But after this atomic blow-up, no one will be able to do any warning—and they'll not know what line of research these people were taking."

"Yes," said Tansie uncertainly.

"Then, in order to bring it all out in the clear and the open, they must repeal their laws that throttle and forbid research. This will make Blaine's world less divergent."

He reached forward with his temperon-clad glove and took firm hold of the temperon sample in the "Real" world cyclotron.

During the boiling, coruscating roar of the atomic hell, Tansie held her breath. The ship was driven away before she spoke.

"Temperon again," she said. "Isn't that likely to cause another 'time-split'?"

He shook his head. "No," he said. "'Time' splits only when there is two very definite possibilities for a future. Individual and minute acts such as might be called a major catastrophe on earth do nothing to disturb the 'temporal' advance. You see, Tansie, Man is an animal possessing free will, and he can do as he pleases. But his every act is based upon his past experience, and therefore whatever he does is reasonably predictable. Therefore, while it is possible to state that a tree might grow in two possible ways, the fact is that it grows only one way and therefore we have no multiplicity of worlds of probability. There is no Wheel of If."

CHAPTER 10

"But what about the people who were running that thing?" asked Tansie.

"Tough," said Ackerman, "But better them than—"

"No," said Tansie, taking his arm and shaking it pleadingly. "Not murder, Les."

"Okay," he said. "But you are making me a lot of trouble. By insisting, I mean."

"How?"

"Watch," he said. He drove the "time-space" ship back towards the "past", and stopped it previous to the explosion. He plied the projector in the operating chamber of the cyclotron, and two people solidified and came to the unreal world. "Meet Calvin and Laurie Blaine," said Ackerman.

Tansie gulped and sat down hard.

Calvin Blaine blinked and said: "How did this come to be?"

Ackerman shook his head tiredly. He handed Blaine the several sheets of typescript. "Here," he said. "This gives you enough information for a beginning. Once you grasp the situation, you are to do the job outlined on the last four pages."

He turned to Tansie. "Drive the ship to Barry Ford's world, while I try to explain what's to be done."

"What are you going to do?" she asked him.

"There's some strings still untied," smiled Ackerman, who was now master of the situation and worthy of the name of Great Physicist. "The Blaines are going to build me my laboratory!"

He left Calvin and Laurie in the familiar woods of Wisconsin on the other world, complete with his projector and the plans. Then down through the "time-space" he and Tansie went, on that world, to an era which Ackerman knew to be the critical "time".

"We 'pushed' there," he said. "Now we pry here."

"What kind of measure comes here?"

"Same prescription," said Ackerman, reaching for his temperon-clad glove.

"And is this where the Ford-Laplane outfit comes in?"

"No. Since this is the world of free research, the cyclotron laboratory will be remotely controlled and unattended; no one will get hurt."

"But I don't understand how the same cure works on both worlds," complained Tansie.

"Very simple. The other world didn't know what one another was doing because everybody was afraid to talk. In this world no one knows what his neighbor is doing because, with everybody doing it, there is too little correlation of effort. No one has to ask anybody's permission to tinker, and so when this laboratory goes up, again no one will be quite sure of what caused it."

"But those who were running it will," objected Tansie.

Ackerman smiled. "Tansie Lee is one of my favorite cooks," he told her. "She's been cooking for years. And would Tansie know what happened if she mixed up a batch of baking powder biscuits out of her grandmother's old tried and true recipe—used in the family for years—and when she popped them in the oven to cook, they exploded and destroyed the end of the house?"

"So?" she smiled. "You're going to take a standard experiment and fudge it up?"

"Yup," he said with a grin, waving a bit of temperon, held in his temperon-clad glove.

Again the explosion boiled skyward, and the flame and the blast seared the eyeballs and battered at the eardrums. Then it was over, and they were gone again.

"And now?" asked Tansie.

"Now we effect the coalescence of two worlds of probability," he told her.

Les Ackerman drove the "time-space" vehicle at a head-long pace into the "future". He nodded with satisfaction when he noted that the destruction of Calvin Blaine's world was not to be. And though he had never seen the opposing success in probability—the destruction of the world of free research—he knew about when its probable destruction took place. He watched, and was gratified to know that his acts had averted the successful culmination of either side's plans for conquest.

On through "time-space" went Ackerman and Tansie Lee, across the years until it was apparent that the twin worlds of dual probability were, indeed, coming closer together. For as Les explained it, when the world of throttled research opened up, and the world of too-free research closed down, they began to become more and more like one another. So they were coming closer together not only in attitude, but in "space" as well.

Slowly and ponderously they came together. It took years from the initial tangential contact to where their surfaces were almost in perfect register.

And Ackerman sought through the doubled-world again and found running the "time-space" vehicle difficult because the congruency of the two worlds made through-passage impossible. But across the world he went, even so.

And he found what he was looking for. In both worlds, men were working on research problems. It was a crazy scene; the laboratories were in excellent register, and appeared as one. The men, of course, were free to move, and they were not performing the same acts. It made for a blurring, maddening scene to watch men working furiously in a large laboratory and working *through* one another.

Then one man in each world turned from his work and held up a sample. They were about eight feet apart in space.

Their fellows stopped work also, and each group went below.

"Now," said Ackerman, "if we're lucky—"

"This," said Tansie Lee, "is where we part."

"Part?" he asked in wonder.

She nodded. "I am going—back—to you—my husband. After all, Lester, we have yet to meet for the truly first time. That is—well—I mean I can't very well marry you twice in 'time', you know. You'll have to make the acquaintance of Tansie Lee for the first time, too."

"When do we part?"

"As soon as you are successful."

"I'll be looking for you," he said. Then he stopped short, standing in the hallway of the laboratory as the men trouped past—through—the two of them on their way to the cyclotron chamber below.

He took her by the shoulders and turned her to face him. "I can kiss a married woman," he said, "with a free mind so long as she is married to me."

She went into his arms to be held—as she was holding him—close. Ackerman more than half expected another interruption, but it did not come. That annoying thought faded as he found his entire attention held by the softly eager woman in his arms. Long, tender, silent moments passed, and then returned reality.

"I like your looks," he told her. "And that was a temporary good-bye. I'll be most careful not to make any mistakes."

Tansie's eyes were shining brightly but she merely nodded and said only: "Auf wiedersehen, my darling."

Ackerman turned and hurried down the laboratory steps with Tansie behind him. They arrived just as both technicians were placing the samples to be bombarded in the cyclotron—one in each world but in perfect register. Ackerman stood in the room beside the big machine as the others left, his temperon-clad glove poised over the congruent samples.

Then and only then he saw the rest. They came hurriedly, fearfully. But not in hatred of one another.

Calvin Blaine shook his head. "You should not have done this," he said.

"But it is done," added Barry Ford. "Now he must have perfect co-ordination, or else."

Tod Laplane shrugged. "If he coalesces these twin worlds at the wrong 'time', there will be the damnedest celestially cosmic explosion since the beginning of the universe."

Louis Ford said: "Maybe that's how the universe really started."

Laurie Blaine shook her head. "Don't be a pessimist," she said. Then she turned to Ackerman with pleading eyes. "Please be careful," she said. "After all, you haven't met Tansie Lee yet; and I am your woman, Lester."

Joan Laplane, as attractively dark as Laurie Blaine was beautifully blonde, stood beside the other girl. There was no sign of scorn, nor even embarrassment between them, and she added her bit to the moment: "You'd not destroy a world for the love of a woman, Lester. That's commendable.

I've not mentioned how I felt because of reasons known to both of us. But," she said to Ackerman, but facing both Tansie Lee and Laurie Blaine, "until Lester places a wedding ring on some girl's finger, I'm considering myself as active competition."

Tansie laughed confidently. "Dream on," she said, "but remember, I'm the one he'll marry."

"That's only a good probability," said Laurie. "But no certain thing."

"Shut up," said Calvin Blaine. "This is no time to get his nerves on edge. Ackerman, don't do it. Let these worlds diverge again, and go on whole."

Ackerman shook his head. "Can't be done," he said.

Then the cyclotron started beside him, and a stream of bluish haze surrounded the target and the sample. Ackerman timed it, and then clamped his hand down hard on the bit of temperon in the machine....

There was a solid wave of sound, and a torrent of sheer energy that stormed at them. The earth shook in a series of abrupt shocks, and from somewhere there converged a film of shimmering something that marked the boundary of a field of energetic force. It came closing in, and disappeared within the bit of temperon. That much Ackerman saw before he blacked-out completely, shaken with pain.

But this was no atomic explosion. Instead of sending the laboratory skyward in a billowing cloud of energetic particles, the force of the blast was confined to the space within the cyclotron room.

And then the energy that was compressed by the spherical shell was driven into the "past"—into the era of "fissioned-time". That period needed that cosmic energy in order to function at all.

The cycle was ended, the story finished. Ackerman had started the fission, and had effected its end.

The cyclotron workers, all unknowing, had coalesced; had become a single probability again. They entered, and found Ackerman lying there.

It never was explained to their satisfaction. Nor could they understand why and how he managed to be in the cyclotron chamber during a bombardment without getting badly irradiated. Ackerman accepted their help and their solace for his aches, but said no more.

He started to leave the laboratory, and he was very thoughtful. He alone of them all was here. The Fords, Laplanes, and Blaines were all gone inexplicably—possibly back into the realm of unreal "time". That meant that the Blaines went back to their laboratory to be—

Not necessarily. Forewarned is forearmed and Ackerman had no proof that they were in the explosion. They could not stop the blow-up, but they could, and probably would, leave for safety so soon as the time-conservation-energy factor returned them.

But even so, Ackerman was sorry. Sorry, and yet glad. For his possible woman-trouble had gone along with the trouble with the time-split.

He looked out of the door and saw—

Tansie Lee!

"Tansie!" he shouted.

He ran—and crashed through the glass of the door, landed on the sidewalk in a welter of broken glass. She turned. "Impulsive, aren't you?"

"Tansie!" he breathed, reaching for her hands.

"That is my name," she said, "But who are you?"

"Les Ackerman," he told her. "And you'll be seeing a lot of me!"

She smiled. "Come and tell me about it," she said. She looked up at him leadingly—and for the first time, Lester Ackerman noticed that her eyes were as blue as any blonde's—Laurie's, for instance, but her complexion was definitely brunette, as dark as Joan's. Her auburn hair was—about halfway between.

He linked arms with her. "This," he said, "is probably the best of all probable worlds."

Epilogue—

The woman moved from her husband's arms and faced the vehicle with distaste. "I hate to go," she said.

"You must," he told her. "And quickly, or there will not be enough power to penetrate the 'Real World' back to the 'fissioned-time'. I'd send someone else, but no one but you and I can go through 'time' to the dual worlds."

She nodded unhappily, and started the machine. It disappeared instantly, leaping the "time" between now and the "time" of fissioned probability, where such a machine could easily function. It was back immediately, and she hurled herself tearfully into her husband's arms.

"I've muffed it terribly," she sobbed.

He stroked her head, and then seated her on the ground beside the machine. He got in, disappeared, and also returned instantly.

"There," he told her. "And that is that."

He lifted her from the ground, put his arm about her lissome waist, and walked her to the house, leaving the machine.

Tomorrow he would dismantle it. It was the only one of its kind, and its usefulness was over. Finished, washed-up, obsolete. After a total Real Operating Time of less than ten milliseconds.

But during which time it had really been around!

www.ingramcontent.com/pod-product-compliance
Lightning Source LLC
LaVergne TN
LVHW041748190726